THE
X
LOVE

By
Fairy
Iatlotl

When All is Said and Done. It is only you who remains.

This is dedicated to the times when we feel and think of things that would morally sound abhorrent and terrifying.

Prologue

"Why are these stupid kids wearing nighties in broad daylight and that too to school?" El Samson; the reporter asks while biting into her mayo dripping burger.

"Yea its crazy"; Valkz replies editing last night's clip on the van's computer. "Heard some crazy popular girl wore it in some party and since then it's a trend at school"; he sighs; "Fuckin' teenagers"; he mutters under his breath.

"And here I thought my high school was the freaky hollow"; El chews on her burger. Her eyes scan around each and every child entering the school premises.

"Again, why are we at this?" Nargis drops her video recorder and peeps back inside the van; "I mean, am all in looking at those lacy nighties all day, but I don't explicitly understand how will that help us getting bites for the Enoch disappearance case?"

"It's the girl"; El takes another bite.

"The girl with the witch-town name. She goes here. Adam Enoch was her father"; El speaks with her mouth all full. Nargis makes a disgusted face.

"Salem?" Valkz looks away from the computer and adjust his spectacles. "Yea that w-un!" she points with the finger she holds her burger as she fills her mouth with it.

"Please, just keep your mouth shut until you're done with your burger"; Nargis convulses in repulse. El shrugs and rolls her eye and takes another bite of the burger.

"Fucking hate high school!" Valkz turns back to his computer.
"I love it!" El is finally done with her extra large burger and wipes her fingers.
"It's all gossip and mania if you ask me"; she smirks.

Some days ago

Vixxi – 1

This is a cautionary tale. A tale that needs to be heard and told and heard again until people start realising the purposelessness of life. How worthless it is! But wait; do not be carried by the statement. Life maybe accidental and absolutely purposeless but is not unromantic. Romance is the essential ingredient to a memorable life. Romance is what made Keats write and Wordworth see in the green of nature and in the blue of the sky. Romance is what made Napolean see in the red of blood an invincible victory. Romance is what made Mark Anthony summon loyalty for Ceaser. Romance is the tragically stupid confusion that killed Romeo and Juliet. And sadly for the characters here, Romance is the turning point of their life. Romance is what inspired Salem to befriend Orleans and together they made the most terrifying of deals. Romance is what converts hate into revenge. Romance is what disguises desperation with love. Romance is what punctures reality.

And this story is a romance. The most dangerous romance. The kind of romance that will let you justify the hellish acts of Salem and Orleans. This is their story and this story is their romance.

Episode 1: Orleans

To meet him was a Miracle.
To know him was God.

I knew that one day when I'll meet someone worthy of falling in love with, these words will become my exact utterances. My heart, my brain, my feelings, my hormones, my thoughts and even my flawless dusky caramel chocolate skin will radiate the effect of these utterances. The holy spirit would itself descend upon me and channelize such powers in me that my vessel would burst into flames.

"You do realise that is sex that you are writing wandass";

Urgh! The peephole is here again!

I shut my diary immediately. Writing openly is never good, I should have known. My tongue twists around in my mouth and my eyes droop as I lift my face to see the most gorgeous face on the planet. Urgh! The Mighty Pain in the ass. The Glamour of the school. The Beauty of Cauldwichh High. The Magnificent – the one and only – the sole heir to the Enoch throne – Salem Enoch.

In front of her, the world is a blib; "Mind your fucking business goldshit"; I take my tongue out and express my inner most gratitude.

"Cannot"; she rolls her eyes and takes a seat next to me with her perpetual love : the biology book in her hand.

"Excuse me?" I raise my eyebrow, candidly and very shamelessly express how much unwanted is her presence to me.

 But of course; the Queen of Glamour is either dumb to receive the hint or dumber to ignore it.

Why can't she get that I wanna sit alone on the bench and relieve my eyes by watching the boys on the field?

"Salem, to make things clear, I like air around me clear, so if you would just scoot and leave me and my peaceful vanilla scented bubble alone it would help me unpollute the air for me"; I smile intensely and unnecessarily.

Salem bats her eyelashes at me and pouts. It looks like she is coming up with a savage reply but interestingly she licks her lower lip, heaves a sigh, open her book and lowers her head into it.

This is outrageous! I hardly like to interact with people let alone let the snobbish little black headed capitalist princess sit next to me. I press my lips tight and jerk my head upwards looking at the roof dramatically.

This is my style for summoning immense anger; it's like if there is a biographical (or autobiographical) movie made on me I would like my character rich with traits. It's my way of moulding, building and intensifying my character. To some it may just be a pathetic deal of dramatic shit, but for me, it is my life; I like to give my actions a meaning; I like to believe that each step of mine is being counted, I like the fact that superstitions can help me relate to someone and I love the fact that all this gives a purpose to my existence. As if I was born to be me.

Except for one thing.

Oh! I hate that thing; I hate the very fact that I am that thing.

I cannot reveal.

The sole reason to curtaining it is the fact that it has no reason to be revealed.

No point for my audience to know what that thing is. No point for my audience to judge me, or to label me with a tag.

And no, it's not my sexuality.
And no, it's not my ethnicity.
And no, I did not kill Mr. Roe's dog. (Well – atleast not intentionally and consciously, I was unaware that chocolate could kill dogs.
I mean, that's just sad – it's better to be dead than never taste chocolate. That is pure sin.)
Right now, all one needs to know is that I am sixteen, my name; Orleans and I have a big – no – massive – no – humungous crush on Marco; the hottest and the most incredibly beautiful boy on the planet.
But coming back to the real time reality; I summon my anger and growl under my breath. I get up, leave my seat and move down to a lower bench and just as I leave the platform where I was sitting a minute ago I release my anger.
A little wave of my fingers does the trick and poor Salem's bench cracks open and she goes down and down and down the pit hole of the spectator benches.
You see – that is my big secret.
I guess now it does have a reason to be revealed. The commotion produced is massive. Everyone turns around and looks in my direction. I can't stop but laugh incessantly. In my defence I did warn the pathetic creature.
I look down the pit hole and find Salem hanging by one of the bench holder wooden limbs that support the higher benches.
Salem looks upward and narrows her eyes at me. Even that didn't stop my smile, all I could do was stifle it for decency.
"I will kill you Orleans"; she mutters before people come running to her.

"Oops!" I laugh.

Episode 2: Salem

"You have to lose your pelvic fat Salem, it can't even stay against gravity!"
My mother's flawless unwanted opinion rings through my ears as I sit in the car. I look at her, her glasses were on. A possible shame must be evidently burning her eyes shaded by her immaculate Giorgio Armani.
"Thank you so much for the concern"; my words carried what my voice tried not to – sarcasm.
"Don't act witty – the bench won't fall down on its own, thousands of girls were sitting there, none of their seats cracked open – ";
"Mom please!" I try stopping her from the predictable rant.
"– It is all my fault! Neither had I married into your father's family, nor would I had produced such genes – everyone likes a girl lean and petite, nobody – absolutely nobody likes a slouching figure and highly protruding back side"; there goes the roast of the year. This is highly insulting!
"It's not so, everyone loves JLo and she has a huge ass. And as a matter of fact, Cardi B had to get her butt surgically increased on account of big butt popularity – so I guess not nobody likes a highly protruding back side"; I venture a bit of sensible argument. But logic wasn't my parents' forte, especially when it comes from people who are either unemployed or under eighteen. In my case, am both.

My mother is probably giving me her intense stare from behind her Georgio Armani. Her jaw tightens as I sip from my water bottle. The nurse said to remain hydrated as my body went through an intense fall. I have zero idea how water is going to help me stay put, but I guess it got to do with body fluids and stuff. Or probably to prevent a possible concussion. Apparently the nurse thought that my fall was caused by my carelessness; I must have had stepped on some already cracked wood and fallen all the way down.

But I know that's not true. That's complete bullshit. I know that it was something done by Orleans, I just need to know how. That crazed out stupid weirdo – how was he able to pull out such a stunt.

My mother, just like everyone else, was unaware of this. Stupid Orleans! He is the fucking reason why I have to bear my mother's temper.

AAAAHHHH!!! HOW I HATE HIM!!!!

"Stop with all that senseless talk Salem"; my mother impulsively speaks her mind.

"Do you have any idea, your little irresponsibility costed me such precious time. I had to run from my Lit Gala meeting to pick you up when all you've got are some scratches and an enormous amount of shame on your shoulders"; her words are so sweetly produced that somehow they intensify their cruelty. It's a rare piece of talent.

I sigh. That's my sign of giving up.

"I can't handle you. You ask of me to treat you like an adult. But you are so worthless, and useless and such a clumsiness. Oh! I can't even deal with you even for a second";

Believe me the feeling is mutual mother!

She is exhausting.

I dig in my bag and take out a pencil and a sharpner. I am aware that my mother's eyes are all over me.

I can feel the intensity of her stare. I sharpen my pencil. A smile is permanently plastered on my face. I take the pencil out of the mouth of the sharpner and in a blink of an eye, with full throttle, stab my calf with it. Pain surges through my leg as I take out the sharp pencil lead. Blood gushes out from the carved hole. A fresh injury.

"Sorry – am clumsy"; I shrug my shoulders. The wound is too painful to bear; who could have thought a simple lead of a simple pencil could puncture such amount of flesh and produce such fiery pain.

I look at the gaping mouth of my mother. She stays speechless.

"Atleast it's not a scratch"; I defend myself. I can feel my physical pain take over my hormones. I can feel my hurt.

Mother shuts her mouth raises her eyes and look away from me.

"Can't even talk"; she murmurs.

I again dig in my bag and take out a clean white handkerchief. My poor pencil is stained with my spoiled blood. I clean it. Open my pencil satchel, put it there. Neatly fold my handkerchief and put it back in my bag.

I can feel water brim my lids, I take out my Prada and wear them on.

Ah! What a relief they bring to me.

Episode 3: Salem

Sometimes, when I admire my mother's diamond necklace on her sleek, petite neck, I wish to gently stroke it with my fingers curl its cold metallic tail around my thumb and pull it hard; making the sharp diamond dig into her flesh and choke the very last breath as the blood slowly starts seeping out and escaping the sharp collar.

But well... even I know I won't.

My eyes slide back to the biology textbook as I observe the diagram of the Blood System if the human body. I outline the limbs in the diagram. Circling around the spot where I am injured. It feels such a relief to see a skinned-dissected picture of what is inside me. The veins, the blood, the bones, the muscles, the limbs, et cetra, et cetra; all make me feel so substantial, so definite, so composed and controlled. The picture guarantees that I would look exactly identical if I open up myself limb by limb, cell by cell.

Unlike of course my mouth.

If you skin my mouth all you will find are my muscles stationed perpetually in upward direction. My smile has no meaning, my frowns even less; just a development one makes around Enoch family. Suffice to say that my emotions are trained to exist in 0 Kelvin emotional atmosphere.

"Salem, could you please tell me why am I looking at a street hobo from a third world country?" My mother; Mrs. Enoch, gives me a threatening eye. I take in a deep breath all ready for a fight.

"It is my du-"

"Mrs. Enoch?" The maid enters and as usual I am left interrupted and ignored. My mother turns around; already forgetting to scold me; gives the made her whole hearted attention.

"Yes Daisy?" She answered.

"Mr. Enoch's breakfast is on the table" She gives her the most vital information of the day. It is basically her job.

"Very well Daisy I'll be there in a minute"; mother answers. I roll my eyes as mother starts to move around the room and enter her closet. It is a ritual; no food ever passes or is eaten by father unless my mother inspects it thoroughly. I have never asked why, or even thought about this stupid ass grand ritual of treating my father as some dependent emperor. My guess, mother just likes to feel the idea of dad being dependent on her in some way. It is sad, but believe me this might be the closest reason as to why she checks all the food that father digests.

Suddenly all this fuss about food and father is taking me on a spurn. I get up to distract myself from my thoughts and randomly walk closer to mother's closed closet. The door is a bit ajar. I try taking a peek through it.

I see her closing some old, probably ancient, wooden case on her vanity table. A pink bottle is kept on its side. Mom stands away searching for something in her drawer and the pink bottle glitters under the florescence of her vanity lights. The bottle is unusual, it is too pink to be a liquid. Mother comes back to the vanity, and I step away from the door. Limping my way back to the room couch.

Now this is interesting; a pink bottle that nobody knows about. What is it? Poison?
"What are you still doing here? Aren't you supposed to leave for school Miss Cripple Hunchback?" There comes another one of my mother's dignifying and over encouraging compliments.
"Was about to"; I forcefully smile.

I follow mother down to the dining table, where Enoch breakfast is lavishly catered. From outside the room, I see mother fill a glass with OJ. That is father's compulsory dose of liquid as recommended by the family doctor.
I turn around as I hear father shout at his assistant; he just entered the lobby and is heading over here. It would be a thundering surprise for my father if he found me here and not on my way to school; which apparently started fifteen minutes ago, so that states I am officially late. And this information might elevate his blood pressure levels and his already agitated nerves.
I turn around again and notice mother take her pink bottle out. I have never seen this. She taps the base of the bottle and a few drops fall down the throat of the bottle and into the OJ. My mother is aware of my father's approach – his angry shouts are making it evident enough.
I quickly hide behind the pillar. My dad's a bad sense preceptor. He is bad at observing; in fact if a kangaroo stood in the middle of our foyer, he would take it as my mother's input in foyer decor. He is that oblivious to reality and his family.

Dad seats himself and the first thing that mother does is place the juice glass in his hand. He gulps it down and suddenly as if on cue the assistant stops hovering around in panic. He is automatically composed.
My father takes a deep breath in and smiles.
"Calm down Raina"; he says but that came as a shocker only to me and interestingly not to his assistant or my mother.
I can feel my eyes widen. Mother bites on her fruit and smiles to herself, happy of some unusual achievement.
My father puts his hand over my mother's and he squeezes it gently.
Now that's massive unusual.
They never do PDA.
Their kind of PDA is yelling in each other's faces.
I've never observed my parents this closely; maybe that's because I've never skipped first period and actually put time and effort in observing my parents have breakfast. Now that I am – I smell fishy business out here. But the thing is – I know the fish.
In fact, now I need that fish.
I take out my burner phone (of which nobody knows or would ever know – especially my ignorant family) and instantly start composing a text message. My brain is storming with ideas; and I – I am concocting a plan.
A plan against my parents.
I walk in as I type on my phone.

"What are you still doing here?" mother raises her voice. I least care. I do not give her any heed, in fact I pass by my father, pretend that I know nothing and there goes my hand pretending to take a banana. And as I take it out from the fruit basket I very discreetly nudge the OJ jug with the tail of the banana and *Whoopsy!*

I start a domino. The OJ jug drops on the milk jug which pushes the dish which drops on the lemon jug and so it goes on and on until the whole table is flooded, wet and chaotically irreparable.

My mother very well soaked in the chaos I created did not notice the vanishing of pink bottle.

And thus starts another domino which both she and I were unaware of and had we known of it, I doubt we'd still would have prevented it.

"You are so utterly clumsy. IRRITATING. DISOBEDIENT. SNOBBISH. AND PATHETICALLY CLUMSY! Hereby, I ground for the next two whole months. Get the hell out of here, I cannot stand your shameless presence. You are an utter disgrace to your family. Get out this very instance"; she shouts as usual.

I bite into my bread and speak; "Nobody uzesh ereby"; I chew as I speak, another act of provocation.

"What?" She shouts as I step away from her and start to leave for the door – really quickly.

"I think she said, nobody uses 'hereby'"; dad is on fire this morning. What is in that pink bottle? Drug? Anti-depressant? Happy hormone generator?

"And nobody talks while eating. That is as barbaric as it is disgusting"; she shouts from her seat.

I turn around; "Goodbye Mother"; and chew, spit and speak at the same time.
She makes a disgusted face and calls for the maid; "DAIIIISSYYYY".

Vixxi – 2

Very few find thunder claps and lightening exciting. It is true that most find it absolutely terrifying and some find it full of warning but extremely few have a nature to find a thunderstorm exciting. These few are foolish enough to step outside their doors and risk their lives. These few have a propensity to play with their lives. They like the music their blood sings when they near the thundering clouds. A rhythm filled with anxiousness but excitement and anticipation. This music makes them feel as if they are a part of some legend; as if some Homer somewhere is singing of a prophecy of a foolish man brave enough to reach out for a life-risking adventure.

Episode 4: Orleans

I'll be honest.
I love ripping people apart heart by heart, soul by soul. No kiddin'.
Am a Nicki Minaj fan and on top of that a Swiftie at heart. I mean I'm basically born to rip people, who cross me, apart.
And yet still there remains a singular creature who is ripping my heart into pieces. Marco Butler.
Ah! The sigh is meant to be.
Marco just passed by me and I know am currently, and indecently drooling all over him. Everything – I swear – everything he does feels like Apollo's poetry.
"Oh! How doomed am I!" I murmur to myself. That is one sad part of having no friends.
But no biggie.

I have friends on social media. My best buddies on tumblr and twitter. We chat, have fun, except social gathering we are virtually destined to be together.
"ORLEANS!"
Did I hear someone speak my name in the hallway?
"ORLEANS!"
Ohkay maybe speaking might be an understatement, but somebody is relentlessly shouting – no screaming my name down the hallway and shattering my perfectly daydreaming and ogling of Marco's perfect butt.
I turn around. Oh! What a tragedy I behold.
"That is not what I left you tomorrow with"; those are my exact words as I see Salem stand in front of me; she is limping with bandages all over her right leg limping towards me. I swear, all I did was a scratch-cut injury to her.
"Maybe you did, you weird punk ass"; She spit on my face. So not like the princess that she is.
"What are you? How did you do it?" She is eyeing me like Cinderella's stepmother.
"What are you talking about?" I say acting dumbfound and unaware. She comes closer and I can feel each and every eye on me. Even Marco's.
But this is not the way I want Marco to see me – timid, meek, withering under the glaring eyes of satanic Salem.
"I think you are being paranoid"; I try chivalrously putting my blame on her. Who cares? She's anyway never going to find out.
"Oh – no"; She is literally over me, I feel so sad for myself as I need to take the support of my locker.

"Oh please Salem, the heat is making you think crazy";
I snicker; I am almost trained to slide my way out from
the little troubles that I create.

"Don't you blame the poor global warming"; she grits
her teeth and her deep black eyes dilate in anger and
frustration. That's interesting. Deep black well like
eyes.

That is impossible. I look deeper into her eyes; I take
her shoulders and put her against my locker letting the
florescence of the light do its work and show the
brown tinge in her eyes.

"Impossible"; obviously taken aback by me sudden
grabbing and shoving her against the locker, Salem
turns silent.

"Impossible"; I again mutter, deducing her eye-parts
and looking even deeper into them. No trace of any
tinge. They are pure black. Stunningly, striking black.

"What are you doing assface?" She pushes me away
forcefully.

"Do not try to change the subject"; she narrows her
eyes. My focus still very much on them.

This girl is making me crazy; I shake myself to get her
nerves off of me.

"Whatever"; I roll my eyes; "Believe what you want.
The reality remains the same. You fucking fell from
the bench all by yourself"; I smile forcefully.

And to make things even clearer I come closer to her, trapping her into my personal space, I look down at her and snarl in the lowest whisper possible; "Never – absolutely never shout my name down the hallway or scream at me in front of my prince charming"; I use my threatening voice to make my point. The voice that warns people off to never cross me. I cannot but help thinking what Marco must be thinking of me – I hope he gets a sneak peek of my butt.

"Fuck you Orleans"; she replies. All my thoughts about Marco vanish into thin air. Girl with black eyes. Girl who is not scared off by my warning voice and compelling eyes. Who the fuck is she? For the first time I stay dumbstruck.

"Ohmygawd! How in the fucking Lucifer's name did you resist my scary voice?" I cannot but give my reflex reaction. She kicks in my shins and walks – limps – away leaving me in pain.

"Ouch! My tissues are fucking sensitive you moron"; I shout down the hallway; completely losing the remnant of my dignity.

Episode 5: Salem

My grandmother used to say that if you haven't lived dramatic, you haven't lived at all. And trust me, not only had she lived in drama but also died in drama. She always fancied the idea of dying in a plane; "On my death bed engrave, 'She died as she soared high in the sky'"; she used to say as she waved her hands open and looked into infinity.

Sadly (or thankfully), I am a complete opposite of her. I am numb. I calculate and I certainly do not make senseless death wishes.

I used to laugh at her dramatic style but eventually I understood her. In the end she died of obesity. We all knew she had it coming. The heart was supposed to stop; the veins were supposed to explode and her eyes were supposed to close. The reason for her death was obviously pathetic but it was sadly chosen all by herself.

"Dear Mother of Satan! Your grandma must be one heck of a woman"

I know that voice; I stop writing in my book and quickly shut it before he could peek a single other word and announce me crazy. Again.

"Why can't you just stop being such a maniac and mind your own shit?" I grimaced as I faced Orleans.

"I can do that"; Orleans starts explaining; "But won't that be predictable and lonely when I can spice up my life by spectating yours"; he gives a huge smile.

"You're pathetic. And weird"; I say in a grumpy voice. He dead stares at me as I ignore him.

"And yet am not writing about choking my mom to death with her diamond necklace"; his voice; high pitched and sharp as it is; become more pointy.

I freeze.

Vixxi– 3

If everything in this world was fair, we might be living in the most unfair world. For starters; who decides on what is fair? And also that's a whole lot of lack of diverse thinking, if everyone agrees on a single kind of a fair world.

Fair world is a utopian concept of elite sentimentalists whereas **Real** world, today that is the reality made by elite capitalists. In a world where life and death remain equally at stake; only piggy banks can promise one happiness. How? Easy: One dose of endorphin inducing antidepressants and ALL IS WELL. But it seems like **Ms.** Enoch found something much – much much much better than a simple dose of antidepressant. A dose that not only has access to happy hormone plug but also to many other hormone plugs – a dose that ensures longevity in effect and more than that ensures execution of Ms. Enoch's plans.

Episode 6: Orleans

Calamity! Calamity! Calamity!
That's what Salem reeks of.
She dresses like a British princess, smiles like a Barbie, clothes herself in Valentino and talks as if she has just won an Academy.
She's interesting. Maybe the only interesting thing in Cauldwichh High in years.
Reason?

Simple. She is the only person that knows the art of being normal while being mad. She is peculiarly the most disguised personality that one would encounter and yet the most warm.

That is what brunette Salem is.

A liar. A traitor. A fickle minded insane little girl looking for her mommy. A mommy who wouldn't give a shit if she's dead or not. A mommy who would rather save her diamond necklace than her daughter.

"Well making a necklace isn't easy, it needs a whole factory to produce that. While on the other hand a child - two or rather even one is enough these days"; she would say

"Or better adopt. A rank higher on social status and a check on being a humanitarian"; and one of her friends would reply with a wink while sipping on her freshly made mimosa, and the company of ladies would all burst in laughter.

But well; the above is just a hypothesis on what public perceives of Mrs. Enoch and what I've observed of her through her little nasty daughter.

The truth can actually be different.

Episode 7: Orleans

"Mr. Axel, if you would quit looking at Ms. Enoch and start focusing on the black board maybe you'll get your bio grades up a bit"; I roll my eyes, noticing how each and every head turns around and starts giggling while Salem grunts in annoyance.

"I disagree"; nobody looking at the black board could ever retain a single thing other than the blackness of the black board.

"It doesn't matter if you agree or not"; Ms. Stacy is heating up. I like it that way. Her anger is in a way fuel to my satisfaction. No reason why.

"That's very inconsiderate of you"; I click my tongue dramatically.

"Mr. Axel, if you do not shut up and keep your eyes to the board in the next twenty seconds; I will take you to the principal's office and show you how much considerate I am"; Ms. Stacy is losing her patience.

She keeps on glaring me and I keep on glaring right back at her.

"Yes Ms. Stacy"; I give in.

For the next whole hour my life had no clue why had I been studying whatever I was being taught in that class. My focus; as usual; went back to Salem's desk, she was tracing the Human Blood Circulation diagram. Typical Salem. Gory Salem. Interesting Salem.

Salem has absolutely everything; she has the family, the hair, the perfect taste in clothes, the perfect shoe size, the perfect friend circle, the perfect grades and the perfect guy crushing on her.

SHE HAS EVERYTHING!

And still Her Highness remains ungrateful and unsatisfied.

I envy her. I envy each and every inch of her. I want to be the girl that she is. I do not wish to be Orleans. I want to be Salem. Everyone loves Salem. I love Salem. Marco loves Salem.

And that is the only reason half of the time I consume observing her. SHE literally has everything.

'Except one!'

My inner conscious again points out.

I roll my eyes on the uselessness of that one inheritance I have.

'You have Magic, Orleans Axel. You are the son of a wizard and a witch. You have that, that Salem can never ever have'; my inner conscious has a propensity to get carried away.

Wait. What's that pink bottle in her hand?

Is that... 'True Love potion from the Collection Of All Types Of Love Potions?' my inner conscious stands red alert. IMPOSSIBLE! Great now she even has that one thing I have: MAGIC.

"Whatever!" I murmur and look away from Salem and the tragedy that my life is.

Episode 8: Salem

"There is only one place where one can get that pink bottle from"; Orleans' bugging voice loiters behind me as I collect my books.

I quickly put the bottle away and try to act as if it is an insignificant thing; "And where would that be?" I smile annoyingly.

"Sand bed of Marine Trench in the Pacific Ocean in 1878"; Orleans smiles elastically and mine reduces in a snarl.

"Fuck off Orleans"; I get up and try to slide my way out of the room but Orleans blocks me.

"You know what Orleans. You should ad for adhesive products";

"Oh I will, after sewing your corpse with a thousand of those pink bottles and selling it to your mother for a million billion dollars"; URGH! THE AUDACITY. I CAN'T EVEN ARGUE 'CAUSE IT MIGHT END UP BEING TRUE.

Orleans scoffs as I fall silent.

"What is your problem dickface?" I cannot be less polite. OBVIOUSLY.

"I know that pink bottle. Where did you get it from?" he inquires with such entitlement that it sometimes makes me wonder the source of his overtly dramatic confidence.

"Give me one reason why should I answer to that question"; this seems a good way to extract information about the mysterious pink potion.

Orleans shrugs; "One word and you will be executed for being in possession of that bottle. You get that?" he raises his eyebrows and twists his mouth sardonically.

"Shut up. That's stupid and only people dumb enough like you can actually believe that"; I roll my eyes.

"And even if it were true, I would flush it down the drain before I let some cultic morons hang my brains" I am already losing my interest in this conversation.

"Yea why not! Make the entire drainage system a love potion ocean"; he gives me an eye.

"First of all stop stereotyping the potion. Just because it is pink does not mean it is love. It could be poison"; I shrug.

Orleans gives me a dead pan look.

"Drink it"; he pouts.

A challenging pout. He thinks I won't do it.

"Last time I checked I was a free person living in a democracy. So stop fucking giving me orders and let me go"; now I am getting highly pissed off by this asshole's presence.

"You are scared as fuck. That you are. You will drink it and all those lovey dovey feelings will come out and everyone will know that you ain't a bitch underneath all that insensitivity. In fact everyone will know the truth that you are nothing but a cry baby longing for her momma darling's attention. And like a pathetic little damaged goodie you'd run back to your momma while she kicks you in the groin and ask for her love"; Orleans creeps closer, my breath halts, my eyes on him, he whispers his next words; " 'Cause in that moment you'd forget all dignity, all self-respect, all self-love, all thought – everything, and give into the most softest of desires"; my face skin burns in the moment and I slap him. Hard.

"What must I say I gave into the 'most' softest of desires"; I smile (genuinely) and think for a second that I have finally got rid of the utterly-insane weirdo. But sadly, that does not happen.

 Somehow I end up against the blackboard in midair with absolutely no voice coming out of my mouth. I am screaming at my highest pitch but not a single sound comes out.

"Never – ever. I mean literally never – ever hit me again"; Orleans give me the mean eye and a warning look.

I nod.

He immediately relaxes and I fall down on the floor. My voice still not coming out of my mouth.

"And also how dare you doubt my information"; the son of a bitch is trying to act all offended. I swear if he hadn't shown me his awesome tricks I would have snapped his neck for just talking to me.

"But since you doubt me and my info – let's undoubt it, shall we?"

Uhoh!

Orleans snaps his fingers and the pink bottle comes out from my bag. Ripping the whole thing apart.

That was unnecessary!

Orleans catches hold of it.

He comes closer.

I am very much voiceless. I still being a tenacious try-er, try screaming at the top of my lungs. But sadly I end up stupidly opening my mouth for Orleans to grab and drip a drop of the stupid pink liquid.

"Ah! Bye – Bye Satanic Salem"

Vixxi – 4

A sudden urge to vomit all your sins surrounds her
stomach. Most of the time she doesn't even know why.
No she doesn't feel pathetic, but she feels so pathetic,
so dang pathetic that she wants to vomit all of her guts
outside.

Beswa picks up the last plate of the diner before she
starts cleaning up the Wonkcul diner. It's already too
late to start on her homework tomorrow. Tears are
about to drop her eyelids and vomit is about to jump
up her throat. Or so would have had happened, had
she not developed her coping mechanism. Her coping
mechanism is very simple. Her coping mechanism is
thinking. Nothing but cruel-vivid-dark-dingy-
horrendous thinking. She was a straight-A student. But
then her father said tata-bye-bye and her mother said
let's try being a runaway. Hence, her ending up here in
these dark alleys of a town. Cauldwichh is her hell,
nothing could be more hellish than a place where
poverty is prevelant amidst the boasting of the elites.
Nothing could make you more envious and hateful
than the jealousy you develop when you see those
Ferams and Enochs drive by in these superfluous
luxurious cars.

You know that you want to be in their feet, you curse
your ancestors for being not related to their family
somehow or at least have had worked hard enough to
provide sufficient financial stability.

"Can't even complain"; Beswa grits her teeth.

Beswa looks at the television, and some reporter is reporting of some country's government crisis. How their country is suffering from a war and a pathetic state of poverty.

Beswa narrows her eyes. Isn't such new suppose to make her feel better? Someone else is suffering worse than her.

Blah – blah – blah! Not gonna help me get through tonight, is it? Fucking a-holes, she says to herself. She picks up the remote and changes the channel to some music channel. Cardi-B plays in the background.

She goes inside the kitchen and throws the dirty plates in the dishwasher.

"Hey, hey, hey – you better pay for all that, boy, if you are thinking to break them all"; Haghe says from the other end of the kitchen as he talks with someone on the phone.

Beswa gives him the middle finger.

"Don't mind him Bes"; Katie comes next to Beswa as she wears her dish-washing gloves.

Beswa looks at her, and she immediately understand how pathetic she is feeling at the moment.

"I can't do it Katie"; she tries her best to let the tears flow, but they never start in the very first place. She even tries to blink a couple more times but she fails.

"Hey!" Katie grabs Beswa of her arm and squeezes it. Katie licks her lips, as she gently allow Beswa to crumble in her arms and hug her.

She gently caresses her hands over her scalp and whispers to him; "Why don't you go to the drag race competition MS club?" she pauses; "Entry is free"; Beswa's head tilt up.

Katie can tell her eyes lit.

Episode 9: Orleans

Hello to Creepy-Nature-Loving-Mud-Dwelling-
Giggling-Snorting-Impossibly-And-Unconceivably-
Illmannered Salem.

"GET THE FUCK UP!" I shout.

"But I love the greens"; Salem speaks in the sweetest voice.

Totally unconceivable.

It is like I've entered a brand new world – where an actual Utopia exists and where candies don't kill you off with diabetes.

Is that possible?

NO.

Because that's a reality that a love potion can only give you. And drugs.

"GET OF THE FUCKING GRASS"; I can't help but shout.

Everyone is looking at her and in no hell's tale am I ever going to bend down to pick up this piece of trash.

"But I love the smell – the mud the edgy feeling"; she literally just sniffed the ground.

Urgh! I shake off the disgusting feeling. Imagine the number of bacteria and germs she inhaled right there.

"Oh! How I miss the Satanic Salem!" I sigh.

"Dude! We need to start practise. When is she getting off the football field?" Qnyev looks at me with high hopes.

"Believe me darling I am trying my best"; I wave him away but I can still feel him hovering around.

"Get the fuck off the football field or I swear to crack this earth and gulp you in"; don't worry that was just a threat. And no I can't do that magic; that kinda shit still five levels ahead of mine.

When I thought of making Salem drink a love potion. I thought of her falling madly in love with some guy or confessing in front of the whole school some fancy love for some punk jock guy who would embarrass her by rejecting her. In a million years I couldn't have come to think of her falling in love with fucking dirt and grass – the one thing that Enoch family hates – LITERALLY HATES – in unison.

Immaculate lifestyle, with a hundred percent sterilization, that is what Enoch enterprise is known for. Not playing in dirt or sniffing grass like a strong dose of cocaine.

"But the grass is so green and there is a ladybird"; her head tilts in the opposite direction, her eyes looking at something in the grass.

An idea pops in my brain.

I see a crow coming in our direction.

I smile devilishly; "Oh dear lord! You are going to go viral"; I snicker as my scheme takes shape. The thing with being a wizard is, crows become your bird buddies.

They literally understand you.

"Get up or see the wrath of Satan hit your head"; I warn the stupid girl for the last time.

But she completely ignores me. She is moronic to the very marrow. I swear am never experimenting Salem with any sort of magic. It will end up with a dead beat.

"Fine"; I sigh.

The crow approaches. I wave my fingers and murmur in a low whisper a telecommunication chant aaannnnnddd *whoopsy!*
The crow poops in flight.
"Aaahhhh!" Salem screeches as the white shit hits her face. She is finally distracted by the stupid ladybird. She gets up, looks at me.
I cannot stifle my laughter. I drop to my knees as I laugh with half of the school on the playfield.
Today will be marked in history as the day when Salem's reign came down to the drains.
"Washroom's that way"; tears can't stop escaping the brim of my eyelids. My poor eyes just witnessed the poopiest and palest of white ever found.

Episode 10: Orleans

Orleans. Orleans. Orleans.
Marco. Marco. Marco.
Corleans? Or Orco?
I write my name on the notebook along side the name of the guy I secretly have a crush on. Actually crush would be an understatement; he's my true love.
I love Marco but Marco likes Salem, and Salem loves tracing Human Circulation System diagrams.
So it is kinda a big Open Love Triangle.
The class ends, I collect my things and drive myself out of the class. I walk down the hallway to my locker when I suddenly halt.
'MARCO alert! Marco alert!' My inner conscious starts jumping up and down as my eyes look at the handsome golden haired face. I blush as I realise -
'OMG!!! HE'S LOOKING AT ME!'

Literally looking straight at me; my chest rises like a balloon is being aired. I can literally feel my face glow and radiate. I can hear the air chiming. I can feel my hair blow. I can grasp this one momentous second in a three hour movie. This is everything. Marco's deep blue eyes; all drowned in my huge black ones.
I can feel love in the air as I close the gap between us. I see his red lips move, one day I'll be kissing them. I can clearly see his lips and cheeks bend as they are about to pronounce my name. I breathe heavily, happy at the thought that he knows me. And like in a movie; in a slo-mo I hear my name escape his ever tender lips.
"Saaaaaaa-lluuuummmmm"
"Huh? What?" I stop; the balloon in my chest bursts, my hormones retire back to their den, my whole slo-mo movie dream shatters as I notice him looking over me at someone behind me.
Salem.
Of course.
I give her a deadpan look as she ignores Marco. She is looking directly at me, smirking with her eyebrow raised.
I know that devil's smile.
"Corleans sounds like you've got a disease and Orco sounds like a syllable pronounced by a species of crow"; she says with a pout as Marco lingers about her and she literally has to put her palm against his chest to keep him at an arm's distance.
I am taken aback.
"You little sneaky bi-" I am about to release my wrath on her that she interrupts me.
"Before you say anything to me, I would like to tell you"; I glare at her bitch face.

"I have a proposition for you"; the little devil smiles.

Vixxi – 5

Ding! Dong!
The door opened.
"Thank you for coming Ms. Axel"; Lindsay Langort
was breathing in shot-sharp inhales. Her eyes were
terrified and her forehead was sweating like it was
about to flood the foyer.
Ms. Axel had always thought how the inside of the
Kappa Kappa Alpha. She used to imagine herself
inside the walls of these rich bricks, now she flings
imaging her son into one of these being fully aware of
the impossibility of it.
"What happened?" Ms. Axel, takes down her giant
hood and unties her cape.
"It is our friend"; Lindsay leads her inside. *Everything
about her is true*; a thought pops up at the back of her
mind as she stares at Ms. Axel directly in the eye.
Ms. Axel; who if had heard these words a fifty years
ago, she would have had snapped at the girl, but now;
smiles knowingly.
"Not everything"; she winks at her and quickly looks
away at the luxurious and doll-like house that these
people believe to be worthy to be called beauty.
"She's upstairs"; Lindsay shakes her head after a few
moments of surprising silence that had overcome her.
"Why is she here?" an alarmed voice hurdled Lindsay.
Redhead Miranda glared at Lindsay.
"She knows how to do this stuff, I've seen her do the
same on my aunt"; Lindsay bolsters her point.
Miranda looks at Ms. Axel with narrowed eyes and a
clenched jaw. "I don't trust you"; she mutters in
disgust.

Ms. Axel only raise her eyes before she passes by the two girls and move forward to the room she is supposed to be in.

Ms. Axel pauses in front of a purple door with yellow placard, on it was written: Gisa Han.

"Be careful, she's acting strange"; Miranda says from behind.

"She's demented"; Lindsay quickly corrects Miranda; "We need your help"; she sticks the last sentence in plea.

Ms. Axel opens the door; a dark, dingy room with a pungent smell registers. Ms. Axel looks at a dark figure in the corner of the room.

She enters the room and as she does, she knows the problem. Ms. Axel slightly tilts and says; "Would you give us a minute?" Lindsay gulps and nods while Miranda just radiates a untrusting stare.

Ms. Axel closes the room becoming a part of the darkness too.

Squeak like sound buzzes in the background, a sad sob like cry. A scratching sound follows. Ms. Axel steps into a puddle of hell knows what – probably not poo or pee – probably not.

She goes to the dark figure and crouches. Absolutely no sunlight shone upon her; but Ms. Axel could see the girl. The girl smells pathetic and her teeth instantly start chattering. Ms. Axel touches her back. She can feel the spinal cord trail down to the coccyx. Ms. Axel takes in a deep breath.

Gisa starts to snarl like an animal; her growl shows her front canines which were now visibly blunt. Ms. Axel stands up and takes a survey of the room. Almost instantly the girl stands and leaps on Ms. Axel's back in an attempt to strangle her.

But Ms. Axel waves her hands and the girl flies back and is thrown against the wall; there she stays suspended as Ms. Axel starts chanting in some foreign language.

Gisa: *gibberish – gibberish – gibberish*

Ms. Axel(decodes and sighs on understanding): *gibberish – gibberish – gibberish* *Translation: You have to eat something*

Gisa: *gibberish – gibberish – gibberish* *Translation: Yes – Yes – Yes I want to eat this child's soul, you, this child's blood – this world's blood*

Ms. Axel: *gib – gib – gib* Translation: How about you and I make a deal, you leave this girl's body and in return I'll feed you with something far better than her soul

Gisa: *gib – gib – gib* Translation: And what would that be?

Ms. Axel snaps her fingers and suddenly a pizza boy appears next to her. The boy registers his surrounding, his one arm is lifted, he must have been standing in front of someone's door the moment he got summoned.

 His eyes widen and he starts screaming when he realised that he was in a dark, dingy and absolutely smelly room, with a girl suspended to the wall and woman standing with her arms raised.

The boy incessantly screams and after a second he faints. The pizza box in his hand comes crashing down, but just before it hits the ground and is fated wasted, Ms. Axel lifts it up with her magic. She darts the pizza box in front of the demented girl and opens it in front of her. The fresh, soft, delicious smell of pizza fills up their noses.

A pizza slice detaches itself and levitates in front of Gisa. Gisa's eyes widen, her eyes glittering with temptation. The pizza seduced her to the point she lost herself to it. Her head moved forward to the pizza and her mouth opened in an attempt to take a bite. But as soon was going to bite into it, the pizza moved away.

Ms. Axel: *gib-gib-gib* Translation: So do we have a deal?

Gisa growled and narrowed her eyes, she started resisting Ms. Axel's grip as she convulsed and lashed out against the wall.

Ms. Axel (shouts): *gib-gib-gib* Translation: DO WE HAVE A DEAL?

Gisa: *gib – gib – gib* Translation: Yes – yes – yes!

Ms. Axel: *gib – gib – gib* Translation: What yes, yes yes? Speak clearly

Gisa: *gib-gib-gib* Translation: Yes I will leave this girl's body if I can have a bite of that that thing.

Ms. Axel: *gib-gib-gib* Translation: That thing is called a pizza and this girl's name is Gisa Han. Seal the deal properly.

Gisa growls irritatingly, she is losing her temper.

Gisa: *gib-gib-gib* Translation: Yes I will leave Gisa Han's body if I can have a bite of that pizza.

Ms. Axel smiles; "good"; and the girl is dropped along with the box of the pizza.
Gisa, like an animal feeds herself to the pizza treat. After she finishes the whole pizza; Gisa falls unconscious.
It's been more than an hour since Lindsay and Miranda first heard the screams coming out of Gisa's room. Finally, Gisa's room opens and Ms. Axel calls them in. Gisa is fast asleep in her bed and Ms. Axel is bending over a fainted pizza boy. Lindsay and Miranda are confused.
The pizza boy suddenly disappears .
Lindsay and Miranda comes to absolute attention. The room was neat and clean as if it had never been ever dirty. And – and it smelled like vanilla in there.
Strange! Thought Miranda.
"Is she going to be fine?" Lindsay asks.
Ms. Axel nods. She comes closer to Gisa and says; "The demons we deal with aren't from Lucifer's hell, all of them, they come from our own"; she pauses for a moment as she surveys Gisa for one last time. She looks up and finds Miranda's suddenly changed thoughts for her surfacing.
"She doesn't need me anymore. She needs a therapist and a dietician who will mentally and physically bring her back to health. She needs good food and she needs to overcome her anorexia".

Lindsay's eyes widen; "Are you telling me that all this time, she wasn't possessed?" Ms. Axel smiles and answers her; "She couldn't let herself eat in her reality so she created this alter ego of herself whom she thought is destructive for her by making her eat food. All I did was let the demon have his way, so she could survive. Now she needs a real doctor and good friends to win herself; otherwise the demon might come again; and this demon won't be like this one, this demon would be far worse and would ask her of her life if it had to"; Ms. Axel warns them.
"Lindsay? – Miranda?" Gisa wakes up.
"Take good care of yourself girls"; and with that note Ms. Axel vanishes.

Episode 11: Orleans

"What is the meaning of this?"
A little quake currents through my heart as a food tray crashes in front of my sight on my table. I believe myself to be a sensitive heart; this kind of spasm-inducing external environment is unhealthy for me.
I look up to see who deemed it right to abrupt me while eating (by the dustbin – unnecessary detail that haunts me each and every minute while eating by the dust bin).
"My lady, you're back"; I smile forcibly (as I usually do in her presence).
"Don't try being witty"; she snarls. But that's not it. She pulls the chair next to me and...
Sits!
OMG!

My head snap to look at Marco's direction. He is FINALLY LOOKING AT ME AND NOT THROUGH ME.

Can't even believe that a stupid fight over a stupid diary and a pink bottle could change my life to this magnitude!

"You're glowing?" Salem raises her judgemental eyes and finds it all okay to vocalise her blatantly phrased judgemental observation.

"Why should I not? The popular table is ogling the table near the dustbin"; I smile (not forcibly somehow); "I must have done something right"; I snicker to myself.

Her already raised eyebrow raises further.

"I am sure people must have told you how annoying you are"; unwanted opinionated bitch. Can't even speak that out loud with hot guys looking at me.

"They've tried"; I hang my smile to one side.

"I'm sure they must have tried"; where is she going with this. I raise my chin in question.

"And they all must have failed miserably. After all, you have something that we don't"; interestingly peripeteia hits me hard.

This time it is me raising my eyebrow and she smiling like the vixen she is.

Episode 12: Salem

People can be so stupid sometimes. They unconsciously tell us their conscience just by committing the mistake to be too social. And conscience to a woman is her self-essence. The one thing that breaks or makes the very person.

And now I know the inner conscience of Orleans.
I know his nerve.
"You dare suggest –";
"Oh yes I dare"; it seems so satisfactory to finally have
the lion in your bare clutches.
"You have no proof"; and there the lion shrugs off my
warning. He thinks I would let him have his way.
"I can collect"; I step a notch.
Orleans pouts, not believing in a single word
pronounced by me.
"Little Salem, you have your brains in a wreck; as far
as I know you must have your phone recorder on and
might be having this conversation recorded. The thing
is Salem; I've met a lot of people like you. People who
are homophobic and absolutely disgusting and can't let
a simple gay man be alone. They'd try to pin weird
things on him or her; for instance like you are trying to
pin whatever that is on me. So please stop. STOP
THE FUCK BULLYING ME!" Orleans takes away
my cell phone and stops the recording on the screen.
 "Well that's a stunner I recorded against you";
Orleans snicker.
I am stunned for a second.

"I am not a homophobe"; I murmur and my eyebrows
crease.
"What?" he looks at me away from my phone.
"I said I am not a homophobe"; I shake myself from
the pathetic blame that I've been just accused of.
"You were making fun of my ship names for
gawdsake! How are you not a homophobe?!" Orleans
looks at me in disbelief.

"First of all I least care if you are gay; second, I was making fun of the ship names because they were worthy of making fun and third, get this through your head – I fucking can be a murderer, an imposter, a freakin' sociopath – but am not – lemme repeat – AM NOT – a homophobe"; I tilt my head and bite the inside of my cheek, and snatch away my phone before he'd transfer the file to his.

"And also, am not a sentimental stupid-ist. So keep your fucking hands away from my phone and hear me out"; I come to the point as I delete the now recorded file.

"I don't wanna be a part of your fucking K-drama. STFU!" Orleans goes back to his food.

"Excuse me!" this guy is such a walking soap opera. Well – but whom I to say! I myself enjoy directing one.

"Well, suddenly if a gay person wishes to ship name himself with hisher crush, it is funny and as I quote you 'worthy of making fun' but if straight people do it it's a fucking wedding hashtag"; he rolls his eyes, quite dramatically. Drama in such magnitude that he almost is provoking me to poke my fingers into both of them. But I resist.

We look in our eyes. I with pride – he with disgust and abhorrence.

Because I follow the protocols of etiquette while he obviously doesn't. Mother is right – those who are born in slums can never understand the rules of conduct.

"You are such a fucking statist"; he looks at me in disgust. I see a glitter in the corner of the eye.

"What?" did he just read my thoughts? Oh gawsh this magic boy is exhausting!
"If you look directly into my eyes and are thinking about me – I can fucking read what is it that you are speaking – first off, my mother doesn't marry into rich sugar daddy's family to stay dependent and a robot for the rest of her life. My mother fucking does a job so that she remains independent and doesn't need to wipe shit off daddy's ass. She's a fucking Mother Teresa! And fucking congratulations that you are such an elitist. 'Cause if your rotting-elitist-of-a-mother hasn't told you yet, I'd like to tell you she takes drugs from those slums that you were just referring too just to stay sane for a night. Otherwise very much like you she's a fucking sociopath. Don't even know that you two are psychos or socios. Probably psychos. How does that proverb go? – oh yea! – like mother like daughter"; he gets up, flashes me the middle finger and leaves me in a gasp.
My cheeks burning with anger as he trots away.
I sigh.
"What a fucking drama King!"
I bite into my cotton carrot.

Episode 13: Orleans

"Ah ah ah ah ah ah... ah – aha – ah!"
Ah! Five minutes of heaven and the whole stress for the day fucks off.
Oh great! I reach out to the tissue paper and wipe myself.

The secret behind feeling great and living a super active and energetic life is masturbation at school (conditions applied: when no student is around). Not everyone has the potential to be so enthusiastic and sound at the very same time. But I have. The reason is not my magic, not some witch's potion nadidahdahdah! – it's simple – it is biological – it's masturbation.

The world's solution to absolutely everything.

Each and every day when I learn the news, the world looks hopelessly tragic or should I say desperate for entertainment. This makes me wonder if people have even discovered the divine gift of masturbation.

Masturbating comes naturally to me (and obviously to everyone else even though most remain). Since last September Marco has become my single source of divine bliss. I have been explicitly loyal to him. I remember it perfectly.

21st September: Marco wore a corporate suit for his first MUN and he – damn fucking rocked it – he looked like Will Smith from Men In Black. Like how is that possible? That's just fucking possible if he is under a constant cover of live photoshopping. Yes he is that hot!

Since that date and that event my life has accustomed to a highly timed ritual. And this ritual, I cherish it everyday. Each and every second of that half an hour between between 4 o'clock and 4:30 I dwell in heaven. The ritual goes somewhat like this:

At 3:59 accurate – am in the boy's locker room waiting for Marco from his football practise.

At 4:00 accurate – the football team enters the showers.

Till 4:14 accurate – my whole body is on fire with ogling Marco's sexy body with his sweat and hot shower hitting his ultra hot bod.

At 4: 15 accurate – I teleport to the farthest washroom and hit my relief within a few minutes.

At 4: 30 accurate – am all ready and off to home.

A pure calculation is precisely the whole secret behind the success of this time table. No magic – no luck – nadidahdahdah!

It's pure conditional mathematics. Conditional? Well for starters there can take place some unprecedented emergencies that could interrupt these rituals. For instance when you find a familiar set of heels next to the washroom in which you were masturbating. You'd know that that's unusual since because; first: this is a boy's washroom and second: nobody – nobody comes to this washroom at this hour. All the students have either left the school campus or use the downstairs washroom.

Should have known this would happen.

I close the tap and very carefully head to the door. Open it, go outside, wait for a second – am all ready to bust her – open the door in full spirit of using magic.

"Caught ya!" I expect to see Salem, but nobody is there. The door creaks behind me, I turn around; my hands ready to use magic again on her.

BANGGGGGG!

Something hits me hard on the skull.

My eyes stay open for a second; I see Salem smiling; her heel in her hand. She shrugs and says something that looked like a "Sorry" in slo-mo.

After that I have no idea what germs my clothes swiped as I was dragged and stuck to the school washroom's toilet seat with my hands separately brown taped and kept apart from each with erasers and cutters in between each finger. It almost looked like I were having a new type of manicure but obviously my luck is a fragile queen who retreats back to its den in times of dire need.

I must say I never thought of this; never thought that my fingers could be controlled by any kind of weapon let alone school stationary and some tape. Never thought that someone would actually stop me from snapping my fingers and by default disallowing me magic.

Truly smart.

This girl isn't just someone; she is a true hate child of Adam Enoch and Ms. Enoch.

Vixxi – 6

At the back of our minds, we all dream of a fantastical lifestyle. We wish to one day live it. But consciously most of us suffer from the victory of having had passed even a single day without freaking the shit out of ourselves.
And when I say 'most of us'; it mostly mean 'I'

Episode 14: Salem

"I am highly amused as to why am I receiving such a sadistic manicure when I should be rewarding you with a smack on your lovely face"; the boy has anger. I must say, I am impressed by his audacity.
I sardonically smile. The heel is in my hands and yet the boy has guts to chit chat away, continuously trying to insult and provoke me.
"Well that's the only kind of manicure I know. Snapping fingernails from their roots. Perhaps the very reason why I go to expensive salons and not do this by myself"; if he can be amusing with words so can I. After all am an Enoch.
"Yea right, the very reason"; he rolls his eyes – again.
"Don't roll your eyes at me"; I narrow my eyes like a threat; imitating mother when she wants to get work done.
"Or what?" see – the audacity!
"Or what? Are you seriously asking me that? I have tied you to a toilet seat with your fingers taped and separated with sharpeners and erasers. You should be licking my heels clean and beg for your release"; this time I get to roll my eyes.

He growls.

Wow – finally I provoke him.

"You should get it through your skull nice and good that I can fucking snap your neck and no matter what my father on account of his dear reputation would make it look like a suicide rather a murder by his daughter"; I smile in glee.

That was very much true. My father loves his daughter for all his repute and reverence in the society. Meanwhile he hardly knows which standard I am in or what school I attend. That knowledge is with his secretary; Raina.

"What do you want Salem?" he looks at me with a clenched jaw.

"You do realise that you can't keep me in this washroom for too long; my mom will come and she will snap you dead without even spilling a drop on the floor"; this time he smiles in glee.

What does he think that I am? A moron? Does he think that I haven't learnt a single thing after having become a victim of his magic for five times in a single day.

"Oh! Yea I figured"; I scrunch my nose as I slowly approach him with a snake like walk. Had he been straight, this very walk would have had given him a boner. Heels in my hands, slithering towards him, dropping my heels, slowly grabbing his head, crossing over his legs and sitting on him. My fingers caress his cheek bone, they reach his lips and I rub the lower one with my thumb. His expression is hilarious; he is perplexed and confused and he did not see this coming.

"It's been more than a millennia that you males have sexualised us. Now finally the time has come that we use our sexuality at our disposal. Don't you think?" I love seeing people at loss.
"You do realise I am gay?!" his words come out muffled.
I smile in an innocent pretence.
I lean into his ears and whisper in my sexiest seducing voice;
"I hardly care";
Had he been a straight guy; I would have punched him for not having a boner even after the sexy whisper in his ear.
"Sa – sa – sal -"; he is still confused.
"Does this make you kinky?" he raises his eyebrows.
He is taken off guard. Not in a million years he would have thought that magic could turn someone on. And I know that is exactly what he is thinking. Being very cautious I do not look at him, I look at his lips and do what I am to do next.
I lean, bite his lower teeth and kiss him.
He doesn't kiss me back for perhaps thirty whole seconds.
But then he does, he starts kissing. And the tongue gets involved. Yes! That's the kind of spice I want from him. Stupid ass.
Snap
Snap
Snap
He breaks away. His is horrified as his face terribly contorts in shock.

"That was fun"; I bite the inside of my cheeks and bring my cell closer. I check out my snaps and wow! I have never seen such good smooch snaps.

"What do you think I should caption it with on insta? People would want to know when we start dating"; I sardonically ask.

He gets red with probably anger or embarrassment.

"I will erase it with my magic once I get out here"; he tries threatening.

What does he think? I was born yesterday or something?

"Dude! Some highly intelligent tech free developed an app call PacMag to protect our cell phones from magic"; I smile with more tease.

"It doesn't work. That's a hoax"; he refutes.

"Oh it does! No wonder why I always wondered why my mother had it on her phone"; I scrunch my nose and smile again. OH TEASING MAKES ME FEEL SOO AMAZING! AND PROVOKING HIM MAKES IT DOUBLY AMAZING!

"It's still fake"; he resists.

"Oh dear darling – if you'd know my mother; you'd also know that there is a high chance possibility that she must have had hired that highly intelligent tech guy to develop an authentic app to keep your witch-slash-wizard gang at bay"; I tilt my head in confirmation.

"And anyway – if you think it's fake –"; I lean, teasing him again, whisper into his left ear; "then why you so red?" I giggle at my devlish little act.

He struggles with the tape as I get off him; laughing to myself and feeling all so proud about myself.

"What do you want?" the lion curbs under the wolf.

"I want you to show up at my place at six exact in the evening and hear out my proposal. And also accept it with a one hundred percent willingness shown"; I emphasise on the last sentence.

"What if I do not do it?" does he still think that he has that option?!

"If you do not – remember the consequence would be fatal to such an extent that your entire community would have to pay"; this time I used my father's threatening voice.

"And no amount of your witchcraft can subdue me from performing the extinction of your kind. Remember my words and remember the capability in them. And if you can't remember; I'll send you your masturbating video with actual unicorn cuss coming out of your pinky"; with that I turn around and leave him alone.

"Wait a minute. GET ME OUTTA HERE!" he shrieks.

"Don't worry. Qnyev is on his way to the washroom. Ask him for help"; I lick my lips and laugh hysterically at my work.

"What! Oh gawd! Atleast don't post that post"; he shouts but with less zeal of terror.

"Oh dear! Already did"; and I leave the washroom occupied with a lonely taped disheartened wizard.

Mother and father would be proud of me.

Instantly I go back to her burner phone.

Yes that's what for my burner phone is – I fake as my dad's hypothetical girlfriend that only exists virtually and on my burner phone. And probably on my dad's secret-text inbox. Sending dad a sexy mail from her fake-hypothetical-admirer made by me.

Ew! That sounds disturbing!

Well you see; I hate being the second choice to my father every-damn-time. Actually that still sounds like he makes me a priority. Let me rephrase that: I hate being my father's last choice every-damn-time! There I said it.

That's the reason why I started pretending to be Amanda a.k.a. my dad's hypothetical girlfriend.

Who's Amanda?

Oh! Amanda's my school piano teacher. She was called at home to tutor me; I made sure that I personally asked her for this.

The plan was easy. Make her come home. She's friendly by virtue and my father's anciently dumb brain by habit believes women who are friendly or as near as even looks into your eyes directly are flirtatious or are in love with him. So, I knew when my bold beautiful tiger-eyed pianist tutor would come at a time when mother is generally attending her tea party and father chooses to stay at the dining table doing his paperwork, something is must to happen.

And by something I mean: Amanda is going to teach me piano with her fingers over mine; and this would require her to bend from time to time, and my father would do more than just ogling. He'd come to share a pleasant chit-chat over my head – completely ignoring my presence in the room. Hence, help me achieve my plan.

Thus; all seemed far to have had gone well; interestingly all my conjectures of my father's actions went pretty accurate. So, after a few Amanda piano-visitations. I decided to go on with my plan. The plan to get to know my father well.

One night I texted my father as Amanda. She received a fully attended reply – or should I say *I* received a fully attended reply.

 From then on, I've known my father's various versatile sides; sides which would disgust me and sides which would make me wanna hug him. I feel satisfied on finally having known him. He finally is human to me. I finally can say, yes I know my father. I know my dad. But the sad part is; he doesn't know I know him much better than I've ever known him. I want to tell him but I can't. And this makes me so angry. Angry about the fact he is always rough with me when am the real me – his daughter; while he is so intimate and gentle with some text receiver – a total fake. Angry at him that why does he chose not to be sweet to me, whilst it comes naturally to him when he texts to this other person. I want to tell him. I want to tell him that he can be sweet to me too – fucking hell! He's been sweet to me all this time, it's just that he doesn't know that he has been so.

I look at the text message. I know a father who is harsh with me, and I know a man who is gentle with me (virtually). Can't believe both can be same, all I did is make him think that he is talking to a different person. So...

Well that is the whole story to why I am fake pretending as his text girlfriend.

And I do agree that that *is* disturbing.

But *Whatever!*

Meet me at the Route Motel tonight at eight

I hit send.

Route Motel is two hours and a town away. Am eager to finally execute the last stage of my plan tonight.

Ping!
Can't wait!
I smile. Now I take revenge.

Episode 15: Salem

Combing my hair is an easy task. You take your brush
up and down.
Up and down.
Up and down.
Up and down.
Down.
Up.
Then Down.
Then Up.
Upanddown.
Upanddown.
Upanddown.
Upanddown.
Downandup.
Downandup.
Upanddown.
Ah!
What a relief it would be!
I cross my legs more tightly just thinking about it.
I rest my brush and my eyes wander first to the
window then to the clock.
It's five past six.
Orlean's late.

Episode 16: Orleans

Death and Life is by far the best collaboration. It gives meaning to the absolute waste that is human productivity.
Thank Goodness I am not one of those stupid hair brained creatures.
Am a wizard.
And that too an exciting one.
Am cursed.
Am a cursed wizard. I am an immortal until I kill 5 reason-potent lives. Once I've killed 5 reason-potent lives; am mortal. But still a wizard. Interesting, right? Maybe. Or maybe not.
Salem has asked me to show by 6 in probably the most dramatic and threatening manner (about which am not gonna think or talk to myself till I am ready to confront the pathetic trauma that I received) (and also gotta give Qnyev a damn good reward – that guy really helped the fuck outta me).
 Am not gonna budge from my bed before 6:15. She had to suck it up – with her fucking high headed nose she gotta suck her ass up till 6:15. Till then I am constructively flipping through the pages of GQ magazine and biting on chocolate.
This month issue has nice and tight Timothee Chalamet.
'Yum! I'll pretend he's the chocolate'
Crunch!
I flip as I take yet another bite. Within five minutes am bored of it. I sigh. I lay posterior on my bed with my eyes eyeing the ticking clock hanging on the wall.
6:13
6:14
6:15.

Time to go.

Whoosh! (vanishes into thin air from his bed)

Whoosh! (appears out of thin air onto Salem's bed)

"Hmm... this is a nice, comfy room I desire"; I chuckle as my hands gently touches the buttery bed cover.

Something pricks my thigh. I slide over to see a bunch of yellow envelopes piled up; "What's this?" I pick up one.

I ignore the sudden voices advancing the door. I open one of the envelopes and go through the letter.

Someone is shouting outside in the gallery.

'Adam Enoch?' I read the name to whom it is addressed.

Someone is really shouting at a very high note. On other days, I'd hidden or would have loved to eavesdrop the fuss outside. But the name on the receipent column was extremely inticing, making it imperative of me to satiate my curiosity.

"Huh! Impossible!" I remain immobile as I imbibe the knowledge of the contents.

Bang!

The door banged open. It takes my attention. I am already heavy breathing that when I see Mrs. Enoch's eyes and expression, I start breathing even faster.

"YOU HAVE A BOY IN YOUR BED?" She shouts as she turns around.

"What? No!" The trembling voice belongs to the ever-so-pitiable heroine. Or not. Salem is standing behind Mrs. Enoch at the door; with a startled mouth and a pale face, looking directly at me. In that moment she didn't see Mrs. Enoch's hand coming and break her cheekbone.

"FUCK!" I drop the letter and all the manners that one should have around an adult.

I swear Salem's atlas must have shifted from its place in the immediate effect of that slap.

"How dare you lead a boy up to your bedroom? You have absolutely no character. Zero face value. Waste of time talent! And now NOT EVEN A VIRGIN! Oh dear Lord! You are not a VIRGIN! URGGGG! I WILL CHOP YOU OFF AND BURY YOU IN MY HOMETOWN HINTERLANDS WITH NO ONE TO EVEN LOCATE YOU! YOU THINK YOU COULD SAVE YOURSELF FROM MY WRATH! YOU THINK THAT -"

Mrs. Enoch had it coming.

She falls on the floor in the most ungracious manner. Unconscious.

"fuck!" This time a squeak leaves my mouth.

My eyes look up from the unconscious lady and find Salem standing with a pointy-hard brush in her hand that was suspended in air. Salem's eyelashes flutter up. Her cheekbones are bloody red; her lips swollen.

When I gather courage to look her in the eye; I see fire in her eyes.

She is Aphrodite herself.

She licks her lip, brings the brush to her hair; combs her hair gently and flips them back.

"I propose to you to threaten my mother; plot against my father and in return take back the last collection of all the types of Love Potions that will help you have Marco fall in love with you"; she raises her eyebrow and a sardonic smile tugs on her cheek.

"Are you in?" She asks.

I look down at Mrs. Enoch. Frown. Gulp. Lick my lips. Look back at her. Calculate the odds. I can teleport back. But what would be fun in that!
"In as in can be"
I wink.

Vixxi – 7

Voltaire said; "There is no God, but don't tell that to my servant, lest he murder me at night";
If Voltaire had been a concerned parent living in 21st century working a 9 to 5 job, his words might have gone a bit this way: "There is no Justice, but don't tell that to my children, lest they murder me at night"
Either way Voltaire made one thing crystal clear: Fear is the precursor of respect. Or in his case, life.

Episode 17: Salem

The reason to tape a cardboard box nice and tight is to keep it shut and untorn so that its contents won't fall off.
The inner cardboard surface of the thick broad silver tape torques round the axis of my wrist.
I catch it.
My thumbs gently run down the never-ending track of the outer surface of the silver tape. I hit the uneven edge of the tape. My nails scratch on the edge and pull the sticky face of the tape off the penultimate strip of the tape. The force makes an irritating sound. I bring the faced off strip to my teeth. My canines all programmed to tear apart the tape. The tape gets a fresh even torn edge.
I throw away the obtained strip.
I repeat the same. Scratch. Pull. Rip. Tear. Gain.
'Ah!'
At last I get hold of an even ended strip.

I rub the stuck tape and pat it. When I look up at him, I like the effect of my words on him. He is wide-eyed and red.

Like a tray of prize I hold the strip of the tape from its end and move closer. My finger gently press against my mother's cheeks and I place the even torn strip over her red lips. Careful of the creases, I neatly seal her lips from end-to-end with the tape. My torn cardboard shut again with me happily out of it.

"Salem!" Orleans is an impatient kid.

"Could you hurry a bit! It ain't fucking art taping her lips"; he rolls his eyes.

"It could be"; I reply and gently smile.

Orleans eyes widen.

What can I say, I simply enjoy startling people.

Episode 18: Orleans

Care.

Care is a nice thing.

For instance; a teen tying up her mom to the chair with such care that when she (mom) wakes up she finds her thoroughly comfortable sitting on it.

Care needs time.

"Done"; Salem freakishly smiles.

And just in the same breath exclaims;

"Shit!"

And instantly puts a hand on her chest.

But before I can ask her what is wrong she pukes her stomach's contents on her unconscious-tied-up-to-a-chair mom.

"Oh my fuck!" My abusing has found new bounds. I have seen too much to get back to decent. Ever.

Salem cleans her lip and looks at me with worry in her eyes.
"She'll kill me if she finds out I destroyed her hair"; her forehead creases deeper as she worries about what her strapped-in-tape mother.
Someone truly said.
Care is genuine.

Episode 19: Orleans

"So what exactly are you trying to do here?" I had to ask.
Ms. Enoch did not look quite in a comfortable position taped to the chair in a pool of vomit trying to get through the washroom door. I did not wish to proceed further with this quest while there were still chances of me replacing her in proximal future.
Bang * Bang* *Bang*
"What does it look like?" She tries to drag the chair inside the washroom, incessantly forcing the whole body and the chair through the door.
Mathematically, getting those two things together through that door would only be possible in an alternative reality with relatively more flexible dimensions.
Bang *Bang* BANG!*
"Damnit! You'll have her head off"; the scene was too unnerving for me to stay silent any longer.
"If you have a better way to put her through that unexpectedly tiny door then please do tell"; she sarcastically looks at with her hands on her hips.
She is ruthless.

"First of all who even asked you to tape her to that – that humungous piece of chair"; no kiddin' that thing was highly embroidered and extremely unnecessary with its stallion like back. I mean – it's a chair. It would do its work with or without such intricate and extensive designing.
Apparently for Enoch family that isn't it.
"And secondly there is a condition in physics called tilting-will-get-you-through-tiny-spaces"; I give the stupid-girl shrug. And I guess I shouldn't have had. She glares at me and contorts her lips in such a manner that her disgust is impossible to ignore.
"Lifting a 140 pound woman along with a 1000 pound chair in a tilted position by 134 pound is something that my brain didn't think of. Apparently only you who has just sighed 150 million molecules of air is intelligent enough"; She is screaming hell's fury.
"To be really honest –"; I must defend myself.
"None of that is even remotely accurate, but alright I got the idea and I'll help you"; I quickly complete my sentence before her flaring nose would start breathing flames.
I leave the foot of the bed and move forward.
"I first need to know the proposition that you so intently were hell bent on telling me"; my words aren't suppose to excite her, but yet for some reason her eyes shine like the naughty Lucifer finally received the Almighty's throne.

Episode 20: Salem

"I asked you to tell me the proposal, not narrate a story"; Orleans is a natural irritant.

This makes my work easy.

Like super easy.

"Yes, I know. That is exactly where am heading at. If only you'd increase your patience and bear with the story"; I smile at him, knowing very well that this will irritate his hair to their roots.

"Why can't you be straight forward for once"; see – super easy to irritate him.

"Because that's not the Enoch way"; I reply looking away from him and at my work.

"Yea right, the Enoch way is to blackmail a completely innocent person, send creepy kinky emails to your own father and shampoo your mother's hair while she's unconscious and tied – oh no – tightly taped to a chair in the shower"; his words carry a heck load of intense sarcasm that even if I would wish to ignore, I couldn't.

I therefore, ignore.

My eyes focus on my fingers as I massage my mother's skull. She never touched me there. My skull, you know.

She never grabbed my nape like I am grabbing right now; but she was always interested in my hair.

"Tie your hair Salem"; "Dress your hair Salem"; "You need to oil your hair Salem"; "Get a hair treatment Salem"; "Such dry hair Salem"; "You don't have my hair genes Salem"; "You'd need a hair transplant in your future Salem"; "Blah blah blah hair Salblah"

The thing is I know mother cared for me. And she wanted me to look nice and fresh 24/7. I mean I did try looking nice. But she wanted me like a model straight out of some magazine. Like she herself was. In her youth she looked like a paegent queen each and every minute of each and every day. I could never compete her.

I blame technology for it.

Had snapchat filters and Instagram filters not provided us with their efficient photoshopping, I would have spend much – much much much time on myself. Making me look like a real life model rather a virtual goddess.

Whatever. I still believe that my mother deserves a better daughter. But here's the thing.

I deserve a much much much much better mother.

"So where was I?" I look back at the leaning Orleans; he is extremely interested in my letters.

"What exactly are they?" he looks at me with a disgusting face.

"They are the story"; I shrug with an 'obviously' expression in my gesture.

Episode 21: Orleans

Looking at Salem and her taped mother under the shower is one disturbing sight. On top of that reading the contents of these letters feels like the sourest cherry on top of the stalest cake.

Salem is washing her vomit off Ms. Enoch's hair and chest as if she's caressing some coma stricken woman or as if one caresses his doll. I am telling you – it's a disturbing sight.

"So the story goes like this: Once upon a time; there lived a rich, beautiful and overachieving girl with rich, beautiful and overachieving parents in a rich, beautiful and overachieving mansion - ";
"Sounds like a story I know"; I pout in disappointment.
"Oh – that is what everyone thinks"; she smiles and turns off the hand shower. She takes the shower towel and starts drying her mother.

Episode 22: Salem

"Everyone thought that they were living a happily ever after. But they weren't. In fact they were living a frustrated-ly ever after. None of the members were ever satisfied with each other. And especially their little girl seemed to them an annoyance. Annoyance for several reasons. First and the foremost: she was the singular reason why the father did not take a divorce with the mother. As it happens according to their prenup; if a child was born out of marriage the billion industry was to be divided 60-40. Sixty goes with the mother and the child while forty goes with the father. At the time of its making; this seemed as a logical divide. But only after the father realised that the Sixty would remain with the mother until she believes her child responsible enough to hold her 40 percent divide in the sixty percent share -"; Orleans raises his hand; his eyebrows are stitched together in confusion.

"Can I just say – am confused; why is property discussion and prenup details such an important part of this unromantically bland story"; Orleans asks. He evidently cannot resist the questioning of this insignificant aspect of the story. But as it happens it might turn into being the most important aspect of a story.

"Well – without it, you will not understand the reason behind the beautiful and tempting proposition that I am to make in a few minutes"; I reply as politely as one does in a business deal. Another one of the virtues I gained observing my parents.

Orleans gulps, tilts his head and says acquiescingly; "Oooohkay"; and exhales heavily. He does not understand the purpose of this story; but I know for a fact that he will like the ending of the story far better than its beginning.

"Everything gets complicated after it. But this did not alter or stop father's intentions in anyway. He became involved with a woman when his girl was just ten. The thing was the girl wanted to feel so many things. Things like hate, anger or distrust. She wanted to feel sad. And to everyone it looked like she did feel all those things.

But all she really did feel was that this could lead her to an average life with a limited amount of money. And this thought scared her. She did not want to lose her closet in her grand mansion.

Or the umbrella of the bodyguards that she tagged along with her whenever she wished to show off her power.

Or to bend herself to tie her shoe laces. See all these things mattered to her. She didn't want to lose all this in any case. And that's when her parents wish came true. She became economically intelligent, competitive and moreover a girl with foresight.
This was the best thing that ever happened to her. She observed her mother and saw how she shooed away the affair like a flying mosquito.
But you see – she also observed that she saw her father and how in flying away the bug that was ruining their marriages; something completely unexpected happened.
 A big editing took place in the prenup.
The editing was a fifty-fifty percent share of the property with T&C of no-affair policy and in which the heir would receive a mutually decided portion when the time deemed right"; I pause and look at Orleans.
I am right; he is completely absorbed in the story.
I am never wrong.
Mother is not drenching anymore. She's wet but not drenching.
"What happens next?" I hear Orleans. Ah! Greedy for more? Of course you are dear Orleans. I think about him just before meeting his eyes.
I turn to him with the wet towel in my hand. I continue.

"Next? The little girl grows. She started understanding the importance of T&C and how she wanted her parents to see her eighteenth birthday as the day when the time deemed right for her to inherit the entire of the property. She started looking at the world in a different light. Unfortunately, her parents didn't share her world view. She was a little bit sad with such dissent. But soon – oh – there are so many buts in this story – Phew! I am already tired of narrating"; I wipe my face with the wet towel.

I can smell mother's shampoo underneath my shampoo. Her scent is that strong. It never leaves her. "A woman's scent is her weapon. It is a signal to your dryness. If it is weak, it suggests you are; if it is strong, it suggests you are too palpable to be strayed away but if it is subtle and just there, well that is a true women's scent. It suggests your invaluable worth and priceless femininity"; her words are haunting. I swear all I wish to do is smack her teeth out when she says those things.

Her kind of femininity is only found in a zoo. A Victorian zoo. Or maybe am wrong. Maybe it is found today too. Hmm... a piece of thought, isn't it?

"Umm – Salem. Are you okay?" Orleans asks me; I did not expect him to ever ask me that.

Wow!

"I am totally fine. It's just the steam and the washroom. It's a bit suffocating. Why don't you get her outta here"; my words don't take him to a rollercoaster ride. In fact he seems exasperated with that sigh he just released.

"You are trying my patience"; he clenches his jaw and gives me a glare.

"I am. Am I?" I feign a frown behind a mischievous smile.

Orleans doesn't get my humour, he shakes his head slowly in disbelief, pats his forehead and turns around with shrugging shoulders.

"Where do you want her?" he asks in an evidently annoyed voice.

"I come out of the washroom and look around. If I take her out; she'd wet the whole place. My beautiful expensive Arabian rug would become a flea market display.

For a minute I turn my head here and there. And then I found the perfect place for my wet mother.

"Get her there"; I point at the place where I want my mother dried.

Orleans lifts his head and look at the place in bewilderment.

His head jerks and like half of the time, his face contorts in a perplexed expression. He looks at me and asks for confirmation;

"The open balcony?"

Vixxi – 8

"Dreams are most profound when they seem crazy"; so said Freud. Surely, undramatic dreams are tranquil, and tranquillity is the state of concentrative inactivity or is it the state behind intense activity? A difficult debate to resolve.

But , one thing is sure. To make the crazy normal – follow your dreams and never give up on them no matter what.

I repeat.

NO MATTER WHAT.

Episode 23: Orleans

I shouldn't have told Salem about my mind-reading powers. That was stupid of me.

After a thorough observation of Salem. One thing is clear.

She is not sane. Like at all.

She acts like a dog with the morphology of a poodle and the behavioural traits of a german shepherd.

And that picture is evil.

In fact I would go as far as to say that she *is* evil.

And had I not been interested in all this drama which I confess is an interest induced by her blackmail, I would have gone far-far away from her and here.

The problem with Salem is that she thinks that she is pure evil. But she's not. She's the most sensitive evil. And that kind is the worst.

These are some serious shitty thoughts that am having while standing above a fourteen metre high balcony. It's windy and chilly out here. I get goosebumps just looking at the ground.

"Shit!" I murmur.

I legit can imagine seeing my cracked and splattered dead body down there.

"Oh boy"; I inhale a deep breath and take a step – several steps – back from the railing.

"Found it"; Salem's cheery voice pops in the background and I turn around to see a smiling Salem with hair dryer in her hand and nicely tied and unconscious Ms. Enoch seated in the middle of the balcony.

She looks like a real beauty degenerate. Unfathomable!

"The dryer? Don't you know where you keep that thingy?" I ask. All thanks to my curious nature that I couldn't keep my mouth shut and save myself from hearing a ludicrous response. But No! My stupid mouth had to act on its reflex and bear with the elitist response as expected.

"Oh, I don't know. Kacia knows. She's my hair dresser. I don't go out without her dressing up my hair every morning"; She informs me as if she's informing one of her elitest friends – casually.

"I don't understand. Do you call her every time that your hair gets messy?" I mean mom gotta hear this – this fashion extremism according to her. Not even kiddin' – my mom thinks that am fashion savvy, she should definitely meet this girl in front of my eyes.

"Oh no, that's the thing. Kacia is only paid for my school time hair. That's one of the major reasons why I have zero control over my head when they get messy and mom goes all Cinderella's stepmother over me. Only occasionally is Kacia charged extra, when there's an outing or someone important visits"; she explains to me as she plugs in the dryer and carefully combs her mother's hair before drying them.

I am amazed. This Kacia chick. I bet she doesn't even know the H of hair dressing; and yet she's fooling this lot and gaining a handful. Or maybe she does know her shit now that I carefully observe Salem nest of a hair.

Dear Mother of Satan! Kacia's a magician. That nest of hair makes me doubt about the whole I-envy-Salem-Enoch-dilemma. Actually this whole night does. But that hair – that's the defining moment.

 "It must be difficult for you to keep them combed, right?" not sure myself if am being sarcastic or genuinely concerned.

She looks at me with awry eyes. Checking if am as taunting in expressions as am in words.

"You making fun of me Axel?" did Salem just used my last name.

Gawd! What am I supposed to take that as? Am I going to be the next one tied to that monstrous chair from some elite market of Middle East Asia?

I'll confess, after witnessing her almost manipulate me into all this I feel suffice to say that I am after all a teeny-tiny bit afraid of her. Ohkay! Well maybe more but well whatever.

"No – technically am making fun of your riches";
SHUT YOUR PETTY MOUTH ORLEANS.
SHUT. IT. RIGHT. THE. FUCK.NOW.
Salem clicks on the maximum heat button on the
dryer and chuckles. She looks horrifying.
Just imagine you are on an open balcony at a dark
night looking at a woman with frizzy, messed up hair
with a dryer in her hand and an evil snicker on her
face drying away a perfectly tied up elderly woman on
a huge chair.
Think about the image and try maximizing the
dramatic evil level of the snicker – or the possible
sneer – on the girl's face.
Terrifying, right?
"You're funny Orleans"; she gives a murmuring
chuckle at the end of my name. Phew! That's a relief.
"Anyway, thank gawsh that stupid hair dresser didn't
use too much brain and put the dryer somewhere
inaccessible"; why would anyone – like literally anyone
put the hair dryer 'somewhere inaccessible'. I do not
get Salem's lifestyle, but I do get that her worries are
genuinely petty.
"Wow! Look at her hair, they look so bouncy and
amazing"; it feels like she discovered the power of
combing hair and blow drying them.
I raise my eyebrow sarcastically and heave a long sigh.
"Can you now tell me the proposal?" I am running out
of patience here.
"Oh yea the story"; she incorrectly speaks.
Not with the story. NO. I wanna know what am I
doing here or what is it in here for me. It's killing me. I
want the proposal – not a self-pity biographical
narration of Salem's life.

"So here's how the story will end"; and here she goes. "This little girl is going to have every single penny by a simple little plan"; Salem smiles as she combs her mother's hair and blow dries them.

"And what is this little plan?" I ask

"The plan goes this way, I torture my mother; get her to sign the contract which I stole from Father's chambers and which states the transfer of all the important assets to me immediately after I consider myself capable of handling them or in case of the current owner's death. After that I will trick my father here into coming here by becoming Amanda. Then comes my messages; through them I will blackmail him into releasing those messages on twitter. He will intelligently sign the contract for me. And viola! I will inheret the whole Enoch property according to my wish and choice and as soon as possible – not the other way around. But there's more –"; Salem is still not finished. That's a big plan and that too a super evil one.

"But – but – but – I will not leave all this to this"; she smiles and continues, showing off her hungry sneer.

"After all the torture; comes your role. It is you – the key point who will help me from saving myself prom being sued by my own parents"; she bites her lower lip; insatiably happy to tell me my role in the whole master plan atlast.

"You, Orleans Axel, will make them suffer from an amnesia for tonight. You Orleans will erase their memories for once and for all.

"And I being the only witness left will fill their memory gap. You see what they will be told is that mother was cruelly injured by father who had violentely assaulted her in a sexual act.

I will remind her how I came to her protection and knocked father away; for that father has to suffer a minor casualty of a head hit.

"Anyway I will kindly inform her how in a fit of rage mother decided to change the asset contract and give me the choice and wish to become inherent of all the assets as according to my wish. Adding to all this, her brain couldn't have had survived the degree of trauma and so so she forgot everything that has happened tonight; a simple act of coping mechanism"; her little evil sneer turned into a big Chehire-wide-smile.

I licked my lips. That was a perfect plan. That *is* a perfect plan. Gawd – this little Satan's spawn is even better than Satan. My forehead is sweating – I can't – I just can't – this is impressive – really, really impressive. I can't even imagine plotting this plan let alone even imagine being a part of this.

 "And how is your mother going to submit to you?" I ask; Ms. Enoch was famous for her endurance. I am sure a simple torture won't lead her into signing these papers.

"Oh, simple mind torture"; she slowly rolls her tongue. In her hand the blow drying machine looks like a pistol that on time Salem turns it on, aiming for Ms. Enoch's chest this time.

"I will simply ask her to sign the contract. And if she refuses; I will threaten her with abortion papers, I will tweet to release reports of abortion and how the poor me learnt the cause of abortion was property division between the children, wife and the husband"; she smiles sinisterly.

"You won't"; that's not an easy thing to tweet and get away with.

"How would you produce them? Abortion papers aren't found online or something. They have to be authentic"; she can't fool the law.

"Umm – my mother did have an abortion, the point is to not actually create controversy but to create the idea of it in mother's head. There will be no tweet; there will be nothing of the sort. But in a hypothetical future this thing would bring her close-to-her-heart reputation down. With the very name abortion; my mother's conservative elite friends would fucking boycott her and with the kind of reason that I'm providing no one who supports abortion would care to fight for abortion due to property division. On top of that we live in a world where the women are blamed for their men's work and a world where the idea of abortion is found pathetic and horrible, which believe me I think is stupider than calling life a miracle; people just can't – can't believe in accidents. They all would rather believe in a world where we are puppets of some superpower. Anyway, coming back to the plan, the complete execution of my plan would only take place when my mother will realise that such a tweet would ruin my father and my mother's reputation and also the whole Enterprises would be tainted simply 'cause of association.

Now tell me; what would an intelligent, smart capitalistic-minded woman who is standing on a fragile social precipice do with such a threat? Such a deeply emotional life-quakening, heart-shattering threat?" she ends with a question.

The story is nicely theorised but it feels difficult to grasp in effect.

"She would either kill you or submit to you"; I answer for her.

"Exactly"; she smiles widely with her teeth showing. She seems extremely happy with my answer.

"If she kills me. Police will find my blog; my personal blog where I have time and again mentioned how much threatened I feel in my mother's presence and three hidden diaries – hid in three different places written in three different years – once in fifth grade, once in 7th and now. Regardless of my death, my mother would end up in jail leaving the entire Enoch enterprises to the board of Enoch enterprise. While if she chooses not to kill me and if she submits to me, two things would come across her mind. One she would wait for the time to re-amend the will and finally have her way by manipulating me or two that she would have to become her child's pet. What she doesn't know is that the worst case scenario is her bright future. And if she doesn't obliges with it; her love potions might just come handy"; Salem winks.

"I still have a question"; I do not believe a single thing. "Why not just use the love potions?" I ask; that's an easy way out. Why is she going through all this drama which gives her an umpteen amount of variable possibilities.

"Well – first of all what's fun in that? I can't let magic overrule my wit. I want my wit to overrule everything – "; she pauses; "and I want to make mother proud of me"; she is seriously is filled with contradictory feelings.

"And second of all – those love portions are going to be yours after tonight"; she pauses. Suddenly I feel rich. I feel rich even before getting my hands on those love potions. This must how business people would feel like. The possibility of harnessing power with just a statement.

"If –";

Of course there's a catch – there's always a catch – and especially if such a statement is coming out of an Enoch.

"If I do what?" finally I am about to hear the proposal. "If you erase all the memories of tonight from my mother and father's mind consequently helping me remove the one and only inconvenience"; she smiles as if it is just a small favour that she is happy to call a proposal. A proposal to remove a trifle inconvenience. Must say I was more excited about the story than I am about the proposal at the moment.

Vixxi - 9

Do not be afraid of the dark, be afraid of never discovering the dark. You only get one chance at life, like you have only one chance at pain, pain isn't that great but it makes you feel you've earn something. Something worthwhile. Something for which you've worked hard for. Something which is not your privilege but your achievement

Those are the exact words of the people born before the generation why. After that, it went a bit like; "I am not afraid of the dark - damn it's the time when am awake... Discover dark? More like marry dark... One chance at life? LOL more like 'NO' chance at life, 'cause am too busy surfing youtube comments... and pain? What do you know about pain? You think it's necessary, we say it's it's our life support - 'cause we are the founders of comma community... Worthwhile? Hard? Priviledge? Achievement? Blah blah blah - Nothing - absolutely nothing - that shit has no sense to us, what sense we have is the sense of being a prodigy. That's my trigger - prodigy - Just pinch me once out of this dream of being a prodigy - just once and I swear, I swear I'll either die or if I survive - you dead bro - you dead"

Episode 24: Orleans

The jist of the longest story of killing ever:
Salem: Mommy mommy love me
Ms. Enoch: Stop with the stubborn behaviour. I'll lock you in the Rapunzel Tower.

Mr. Enoch: No! That Tower is made for my precious assets. You don't understand their worth; so it is better that you two keep your hands off them.

Salem: Daddy and mommy don't love me

Ms. And Mr. Enoch: GO GET SOME WORK DONE!

Salem: Ohkay! I'll torture you both in such a manner that you'd be so proud of me.

"That's strange";

Salem bends down and sniffs(?) her mother's neck.

This girl has some serious mommy issues.

"Care to explain why did you just sniff an unconscious forty year old lady's neck"; Do not blame me. Blame the impossibly uncontrollable part of my brain that remains forever hungry for answers.

She ignores me and sniffs again.

"Ohkay that's getting really weird now"; I say.

"She's smelling like my shampoo"; the kid seems really worried for a triviality such as this.

But then again Enoch world crisis are majorly either about my nails aren't perfect or my business is acting an eco-friendly law suit.

"Ohkay." I pause trying to sound as concerned as the creases on her forehead.

"You don't understand. She shouldn't be smelling like my shampoo, she'll know about what we are upto!" and there she goes all panic-eyed.

Huh? Now what does that mean? Isn't that the whole point of all this? To torture her and irritate her?

"And if she gets to know that, she'll kill me"; the paradox is too uncanny to go unnoticed.

"And she won't kill you if she finds herself tied to that chair?" that statement had this question comingwith all its mighty sarcasm layered.

"Are you stupid or is it the wind?" She gives me a disgruntled look as if it were me who is acting strange.

"Hein!" I am a bit at surprise with her unexpected replies.

"She will be proud of me having been able to execute a blackmail, a threat and a plan. She will be proud of me in the end of having persuaded her to generate a will that will give me all her riches. But she will be totally annoyed and absolutely pissed if she did not scent like she scents. And then I'd have to hear about it for the rest of the eternity!" for some reason, Salem believes that her clarification is as logical to me as it is to her.

I just wonder what would happen to me if I were to born here?

Huh?

Nononononononono!

That is one scary thought.

I shake my body to shake away the terrifying thought.

"Follow me"; Salem calls out.

"Where to?" I ask.

"To find her cologne"; her voice is a bit anxious.

Have you ever heard of normalisation of situational irony? If not. I can assure you, you can find it here, in the Enoch mansion, in the Enoch family.

"Would it be safe to leave her here in the balcony, exposed to cold breeze?" I am concerned for poor Ms. Enoch.

"Oh she'll be fine. That is absolutely nothing. Mother used to ground us in dark underground cells if we disobeyed her"; and once again Salem informs me with such casualness that even my groin hair are standing straight in attention.

"We?" did I hear it right?

"Oh yea! We; my brother and I. He was elder, but they say he died. It was ages ago; he died even before I was born. Daisy told me that his disobedience got him to the underground cells frequently but interestingly he never resisted them unlike, obviously, me. I resist like hell"; she smiles to herself feeling very proud about the fact that she rebels from being grounded in underground cells.

I check my phone. Am I in the right century? Are underground cells still a thing?

Yep Right century, year, date, everything. Dear Lucifer's Damn! Are these people even humans?

"Exactly what do you mean by underground cells?" I ask as she opens the door and steps out in her gallery. She turns around, smirks and (casually – very casually) says;

"Dungeons. Real life, rock built. Hollow. Dark. Sewage smelling dungeons"; can't point if she's smiling for scaring me or plotting to throw me in one of them.

"Is that even le – le – le – legal?" I stammer, my spine gets infinite goosebumps.

She laughs hysterically. I don't understand what was so funny that she found in my question.

"Are you legal?" she replies me with another question. Obviously!

Well – I know she's talking about magic.

I fall silent.

If you've read supernatural history even vaguely, you must know how dungeons and witches don't go along together. Many dead bodies are found in dungeons; many deaths written on the dungeon walls. I do not wish to be a part of such a history. And luckily am not. Well until now.

"You wanna see them?" she raises her eyes.'

Gotta confess; despite of all the gory history. I am a bit curious how a dungeon looks like. No doubt am scared to the bones; but am also – um – um – curious?

"There's also my this year's haunted house sets. You'd love them"; she is trying to persuade me (or trick me into this) to go there.

"I don't care"; she seriously think that her haunted house is going to seduce me to go down there!

"Cummon you'll love it"; she gives her mischievous smiles.

"I don't get it, if it is so lovable why did Ms. Enoch ground you there?" that was a genuine question, which was nicely (not so nicely) replied with another hysterical laugh and a strange-very-strange reply.

"You're so funny";

I DO NOT SEE THE 'FUNNY' PART IN ANY OF MY 'YOU'RE SO FUNNY' STATEMENTS!

"Don't worry, you'll say yes after dinner"; she turns around and her dress swirl in a circle and settle on the sides of her thighs.

"We are having dinner?" That is interesting; as far as I'd remember she called me here for a proposal (to which I still haven't said yes to quite vocally, but her threat makes it implicit and negates my will).

"Well aren't you hungry? I'll order pizza. What do you want?" she asks.

"Pizza?"
"Well yes"; she stops again, and her dress frill swirls and settle.
"Or would you like to eat my mother?" she delivers her question with utter seriousness that it scares me of its possibility.
"What do you think witches are? Cannibals?" I am offended.
She smiles slowly showing off her toothy grin.
"Gawd no – look at your little red face. Such rarity on such an unwavering personality!" I am pretty sure that is not a compliment.
"I am doing pepperoni; by the time we find mother's cologne, pizza will be here. And then am sure I will be enough to persuade you to my dungeons"; she again gives me her shiny-toothy smile.
"Let's not hope so much" I gulp.

Episode 25: Salem

If beauty had a cunning girl twin, it would be my mother.
Everything about her is magnanimously beautiful; and nobody likes magnanimous in beauty. That's offending. But for my mother this very offence stated her power out and loud.
Just like her beauty, her cologne closet shouts loud and clear; "Shame on the people of the world, they can't have me! Hahahaha!"
I am sure that is an exact representation of my mother's cologne closet if it had a brain and a mouth of its own. Yes, the laugh included.

"Where is this place? On the other side of the world?"
Orleans is getting impatient again.

"Well, you didn't actually believe that my parent's
room is going to be next to mine. It's in the north-east
wing and mine is in the south-east"; I clarify.

"Yea that is the other end of the world"; Orleans
scoffs.

"Aren't you an impatient piece of shit!" I pout; he is
one amusing piece of human flesh.

"Huh? What gave me away?" he slightly shake his
head and widened his eyes in irritation and sarcasm;
"Is it you acting so calm while taping your mother or
you blackmailing me into giving your teeny-tiny parents
amnesia?"

Ah! He shouldn't have spit that out loud.

I turn around with a jerk.

"Excuse me!" I pause giving him my intense-calm
angry voice. One trick mother told me loud and clear.
Keep your voice low and your eyes loud. The threat is
not in the words, it is in the sound. Orleans gulps.

"You have all the cards open to you. You chose this;
you are all the way in as you were all the way out. You
chose to not being bullied for being a wizard-"

"Hmmm, I wonder why, oh yea! That's right. You
ruined in the VERY FIRST PLACE"; Woah Orleans!
Did not see that anger coming. But you see that's what
am trained for, being calm and cataclysmic while the
other party completely drowns itself in its own flood of
anger and ruin its own logic.

I smile.

"You chose helping me, just the way you are choosing
right now of being angry on me and my family. Do you
know what such anger can bring forth?

"Well it can bring forth the darker side of a human being and also cause damage to life and property. Now, you don't mean that I call police and tell you how you threatened me into all this and taped my mom.

"Poor me! Had to stray away and knock you down to escape your wrath and contact police. Wonder how the police will react to the information given that you are completely capable of pulling all this with a single swing of your fingers.

"Surely I won't back away from telling them that or showing them; thanks to your impatient angry side"; I smile once again, mom was right. Right words at the right time and you can bring even God down. See that's where Lucifer went wrong. He was more in action and less in words. More in wrath and less in plot.

"You won't say that. You can't"; Orleans is baffled. What a delight spreading terror is. He is all too powerful but alas he is stupid.

"Watch me do it"; I smile.

"Do you really think me that gullible or the people of this town that stupid? Like I'd let you tramp all over me and kick me in the balls while I won't let a shit happen to you?" Orleans narrows his eyes.

"You have zero idea what am capable of"; I murmur.

"Oh! I have plenty"; he tightens his jaw and narrows his eyes.

"Go ahead; call the police. Do your thing";Orleans steps back and confidently shrugs. I shouldn't have told him the whole story. Urgh! Mother is right. I always get carried away with my emotions.

"What are you waiting for?" he looks me in the eyes; this time it is he teasing me.

"Oh that's right! If you call them how will you make me do one of those amnesia things?" he retorts back.

"Actually"; I take a deep breath in; "I can call them. I can use the delivery guy who is coming here with pizza as my witness and have you behind the doors".

"I will snap my fingers and will be literally on the other side of the world"; Orleans smiles.

"Great then be there and see how you will never acquire the love potions or Marco for that matter"; I smile. Orleans doesn't retort back.

Now that I have the leesh back in my hands I can finally hope all this rant to cease.

"Love is a beautiful thing. Don't you think so?" I pout in acute expression of a tease.

"Well to be clear love is more of a feeling than a thing. But how are you expected to know that? You never had anybody love you"; Orleans scoffs.

That hit me home. Nicely and dramatically; so like Orleans.

He passes by me hitting my shoulder with his.

"Ouch! You are getting good at this"; I turn around and open the door to the cologne closet.

"Learnt from the bitch herself".

Vixxi – 10

Destruction is a funny word.
It counts for everything, it costs nothing. One snap of
mind and everything changes. Everything.
And the worst part is it makes us happy.
On some level this is mind's behavioural plateau.
Plateau.

Episode 26: Salem

My mother is extremely fond of ancient craftsmanship.
She likes her most precious belongings to be kept
inside of the closet behind the fake guest/thief-
protection closet. Each door of her closet is made
from some ancient art of door designing. This
particular door that leads us into the most fragrant
room in the town.
"It's Paris out here"; Orleans speaks from behind as
he takes in a long breath.
I turn around, this is strange, I agree with him.
"I am happy that you like it"; I turn around just to have
a peek of his expression on my words. But awfully
interestingly, he isn't giving me any heed. His head is
bemused with the beautiful little bottles.
"It's like a little museum"; he murmurs to himself.
Completely ignoring what I said.
"Stop with all the ogling Axel; we need to get the scent
before mother wakes up and kills me"; I remind him
as I look around to see what mother actually used for
today.
There is silence for some time when suddenly I realise
that Orleans is constantly staring at my back.

I turn around to look at his frozen expression.
"Am familiar with those mischievous glare in those eyes"; I tilt my head as I say.
He smirks.
"What is it Orleans?" I ask
"I will erase you parents memories; help you in doing everything you want but –"; he finally is on board.
But there is always a catch. Always.
"But?" I repeat.
"But add on some of these bottles and some of your father's clothes to your mother's love potions"; he is getting better and better at this. He definitely knows the worth of his power.
I saw this coming. I take a pause; and smile in a familial sardonic.
"If I hadn't known you; I'd say you're trying to rob us"; I chuckle.
"Well, if that's all I can do to get you to do my dirty work; then why not! Of course you can have all that you want"; I promise him. And unlike my mother and father, I am a good girl who keeps her promises.
"How generous of you!" Orleans mocks me.
"Now can you stop admiring around and help me out here?" I bring him back to the reality.
"Why exactly is your mother concerned with what scent she smells of?" he comes beside me and bents to one of the shelves, inspecting each bottle.
"It is very important. She is obsessed with smells. Hell, her smell obsession is so strong that if I don't change my perfume each and every day she's call me a hobo from the 7th street of hell"; that comment is entirely true. She does say those words.

"Mahn! Your mother is a matter of envy"; Orleans says – but he says genuinely.

"Hein? How?" I do not understand how is her obsession with smells makes her a 'matter' of envy.

"How?" Orleans stands erect and looks at me; "She owns this place. Infact all the aesthetic credit should go to your mother. People work their asses off to live one day to have a cologne closet or intricate Arabian designs on their chairs"; he tells me with such admiration in his eyes. Obviously his bemused expression suggests that he desires my life.

I chuckle; "I wonder how much better would you fit in this family"; I reply.

"Oh no – no – no. Don't take me wrong I ain't got shit to do with your family. But the thought of being your close friend and enjoying perks that comes along with you. Well now that's awesome!" he snickers at me. He is not anymore the wicked Orleans of the South anymore. He's like a normal Orleans who seems to have no idea that he goes to my school or hates me or is intimidated by my reputation as the richest and the most popular girl in the school.

"I am not intimidated by you!" and the expression goes away.

I shake my head with a laugh all smeared up on my face. I forgot that looking at him directly in the face while at the same time talking to him just gives him the keys inside my brain.

"I hate to break it to you but I am certainly not
imitated by you. Do not dwell on that misconception
of yours. I am the last person to be intimidated by you
and your riches. My family might lack with it, but my
life is way better off without it. Am just impressed is
what I am right now. Your mother has great taste in
perfume"; he sprays on his wrist and takes a long sniff
at it; "Like seriously wow taste!"
 I chuckle again; "You are like a little brother who is
getting to know about women's secrets by snooping in
your elder sister's and mother's closets"; I observe
him.
"I am not"; he defends himself for a second just before
getting distracted once again.
"Hm-mmm"; I look away.
The door bell rings. We both face each other; Orleans
must be starving; the glittery gleam in his eyes gives
away his hunger.
"Pizza"; he licks his lips.
"Oh gawd! You are excited for pizza? Wait till you
have a look at the pizza guy"; I say.
"Nothing. Absolutely nothing can ever outdo pizza";
he defends.
"Maybe that's why you are inhuman. You do not
belong to pizza community"; he is being utterly idiotic.
"If you stay long in that community, you'd die of heart
attack or high calories"; I break his bubble.
"You have zero respect for both the rules and ethics
for the Pizza community. At Pizza community; the
demand is always high and the customers always
satisfied"; Oh now this community is a company?
Gawd! Orleans can't even leave drama in simple talk.

"Sounds like capitalism and consumerism conflated in cheese"; I retort.

"Sounds like you'd rather put vegan communism over cheesy capitalism"; he retorts back.

"Sounds like you would rather buy into death over life"; I reply and the retort games continue.

"Oh darling, we all have already"; he jumps down the staircase leading to the foyer.

"Yea I know, my father is the one who bought and soon am gonna take his place"; I follow him.

"Don't you think, you dream a lot, Salem?" Orleans gives his unwanted opinion once again. With that I realise, our retort round is over.

"Guess I do"; he moves forward to the door as I say and walk slowly behind him.

"Infact –"; I pause as I land. Orleans stands away from the door waiting for me to answer the ringing door bell.

"I think"; I speak as slowly and as mysteriously possible. My hands claw the door handles, I look at Orleans and pull the handles with force;

"I think you should start dreaming too"; and complete my sentence as I open the door wide open.'

It takes Orleans more than a minute to comprehend what he is seeing.

"Wow!" he exclaims.

This is regular for me.

"Am I in porno or am I dead and finally in heaven?" his eyes are wide with joy.

"One large pepperoni pizza?" the pizza delivery boy spoke.

"You are so kind Will"; I deliberately hired the hottest abs guy in Cauldwichh to be my personal delivery guy. No matter which stall I order from; it is Will who will deliver me pizza and it is Will who will have it with me. It's kind of the few perks that one with no friends has. And obviously he never delivers when mother and father are here.

He is my stallion and the prince charming all in one. He is my happy place; he is my key to the boy's world. Everything that I know about boys is because of him. He stands in front of us with a mesmerising grin smeared all over his face, there is a twinkle in the corner of his eyes suggesting his friendliness, his hair all gelled and crunchy, his abs all tanned and oiled, the pizza shirt wrapped around his beautiful God like waist, his body weight is on his left leg as he leans on the left side, his right hand loaded with our pizza.

"Yum"; Orleans mouth waters.

"I know am hungry too"; I smile to one side.

"Come on in Will; join us in our little pizza party"; Will shrugs and grins.

"Nothing would make me happier"; his words sound so genuine.

Too bad I pay him for speaking that line again and again each time he drops by.

Episode 27: Orleans

What would you do if you have already fallen in love but your heart treacherously starts beating for another?

Before that gigantic door opened, my life was completely simple (well at least my heart was completely simple and sane); I had feelings for one and only one – an irreplaceable human being – Marco. The divinity of Cauldwichh High.

But then, my life turned upside down, and now all my senses and systems(especially the circulatory system) is betraying him. My heart is fluttering like a new born babe trying to take a flight but is too scared to try because the sun is just in front of its eyes and it doesn't know if it should fall in love with it or burn in the light of it.

Wow! I just got carried away there.

So, metaphorically – yes! I am in love with this Grecian beauty sitting in front of me and biting into beautiful cheese, and tearing apart each layer of pizza from its base. Yum!

I lick my lips just like he does when pizza sauce smudges all around his lips. Wait! Isn't that supposed to be ew? Urgh! Why is it sexy and not ew! Forget it.

"My mother would kill me if she gets to know that am eating pizza in her white-washed immaculate cologne closet"; Salem breaks my pizza boy fantasy drooling. I collect myself and blush a little as I realise how much evident am I with my fanboying.

Don't blame me! Have you seen this pretty boy's eyes and abs. Enchantingly fairylike. Oh wow!

"Again why is he shirtless?" I lean into Salem and whisper in her ears. This woman is strange and absolutely extra. I mean I am extra – I like her extra-ness – but this is not fair, even I want a personalised topless delivery boy delivery stuff to my home.

"It's in his job description"; she whispers back to me as she herself enjoys her extra cheese pizza.

"Why aren't you digging in?" the beautiful boy named Will speaks.

"Oh don't worry he will, he is almost religious about pizza. Infact he has a whole pizza community"; I give a rest-bitch face as she embarrasses me so eloquently.

"Do you?" the beautiful boy asks.

My straight lips curve into a smile in a reflex; "No – Salem is just teasing me"; I press my lips tightly and hit Salem's foot with my shoe heel.

"Ouch!" she reacts; I shrug.

"What happened?" Isn't this boy such a cutie; he is concerned for Salem. AWWW!

'Don't be dumb Orleans, for all we know she would have paid him to be concerned and caring too' the rational, boring Orleans opens his mouth.

'I beg to differ'; says my pompous side; 'I believe the boy is as beautiful as he is caring'; I sigh and agree with my pompous side.

"So what are we looking for?" the Grecian beauty asks.

"Mother's scent"; Salem replies, as her eyes dart away to find the cologne bottle that her mother used today.

"What does it smell like?" the gorgeous lips move apart; I must be looking like a drooling puppy at the moment. I shake myself to put off the beautiful boy's magical charms over me.

"It smells like – I don't know – caramel? Vanilla? Cupcake?" Salem looks in all the directions. There are thousands and thousands of brands all displayed in poise and style.

"Ohkaaay"; the beautiful boy chews on his pizza bite. His forehead creases, and I realise that he just might actually be thinking.

Spit it out beautiful boy. Spit. It. Out.

I am doomed; Marco is going to feel so betrayed if he ever got to know about this change of hearts.

"Well – there is a possibility that your mom might be using two or more perfumes"; umm – beautiful boy said what?

"What do you mean?" Salem turns around.

"There is a possibility that your mother might mix colognes to get a unique kind of scent. Many people do that"; OH.MY.GAWD. Will is a cologne genius. I can marry him right this moment.

"Actually"; Salem tilts her head and chews her inside of the cheek; "actually, you could be right"; "how did know?"she comes closer to him, takes another bite of the pizza.

"I once worked in a fragrance shop. Boring stuff but amazing smell"; he nods scrunching his chin.

"Well, all we gotta do now is make a solution that perfectly matches your mother's scent"; Will says. I nod in a slight pout, amazed by how his body contains all that hot info.

Hot! He's so hot!

 "And how do we do that?" Salem murmurs to herself.

"I guess; I'll get a piece of her clothing. I'd have to rip it. Shoot, she's gonna be so angry about it"; Salem sounds tense. My eyes are well focused on pretty boy's crunchy hair and curvy butts to give Salem any heed.

Oh. My. Hotness. How does he have such a tight butt!

"Why not just bring her here?" Poor Will! Knows nothing what is actually happening here. Salem is never going to bring Ms. Enoch here. Never.
"Oh no – we can't do that"; Salem puts a halt on his curiosity. It must be in his job description to never question more than once. Either that or he has zero curiosity potential.
He takes a random bottle from the display shelf, sniffs, his nose scrunches.
Oh dear me! His scrunching nose makes me so hot. Hot hot hot hot hot hot.
He takes another bottle. I am following him around to whichever shelf his feet are taking him to. I notice each and every muscle on him. He sniffs the bottle, he snickers to himself, his white toothy grin making me feel hotter by each second.
Hot – oh dear lord! He is burning my skin and my groin. He presses the perfume top and the scented droplets escapes from the perfume conduit only to fall on his beautiful, tanned body, landing on his skin like fire shots.
I – am – burning – with – pure – heavenly – sweet – scented – desire.
And he – oh! – he is on damn fire!
He is burning into flames, red velvety flames. And he is screaming, screaming – screaming? Wait a minute, he is actually screaming.
Fuck! He is actually in flames. I don't understand. I turn my head slightly and see Salem screaming too. Now she is screaming at me.
What is happening?
"WHAT THE FUCK ARE YOU DOING AXEL?" she is screaming on top of her voice.

"HELP! WATER! SOMEONE BRING WATER!"
Will is crying in pain. Salem rushes out. My inner
burning desire is replaced by confusion and fear. How
did this happen? How did he set himself on fire. I
stand petrified as Will runs around the room burning.
He jolts for the door but bombards into one of the
shelves, the scent bottles all come crashing down on
the floor.
"No – no – no"; Will starts running away from the
scent liquid in panic.
"AAAHHHH IT HURTS! HELP ME SOMEONE!"
he jolts for the door leaving behind a trail of fire. The
whole place clatters as shelves over shelves come
crashing down.
By any chance is the perfume liquid flammable?
 And as if an answer to my question; the whole shelf at
the entrance burn explodes into flames.
"Oh I better get away"; I snap my finger before the
whole room collapses.
"WHAT THE FUCK DID YOU DO?" Salem
shouts in my ears as I teleport outside the room. Will
is on the kitchen floor completely burnt and drenched
in water.
"Is he dead?" I ask Salem with the dishwasher hand
shower in her hands.
"HE MIGHT AS WELL BE!" she doesn't stop
shouting.
"WHAT THE FUCK DID YOU DO?" She cannot
keep her voice down.
"I don't know. I was just thinking how hot he is and
how hot he was making me. I don't know how did that
burnt the whole place down"; I come clean.
"How? How do you NOT KNOW!"

"WOULD YOU STOP WITH ALL YOUR SHOUTING!" Now I can't keep my calm.

"HOW CAN I STOP SHOUTING. WE HAVE A BURNT BODY IN OUR HANDS!" And she never does stop shouting.

"WE HAVE A TAPED BODY ALSO IN OUR HANDS!"

"WELL THAT TAPED BODY DOES NOT DELIVER ME HOT PIZZA WITH A HOT TANNED BODY! URGH! YOU ARE SUCH A CHAOS!"

"GOSH THAT TAPED BOPDY IS YOUR FREAKIN' MOTHER FOR GAWDSAKES!"

"SO?"

"SO? SHE FREAKIN' GAVE YOU BIRTH"

"WELL THAT'S NOT GOOD ENOUGH!"

"AAAHAHAHAHAHAHAHAHHAHHA!" the poor burnt boy cries in pain. Our heads turn around.

"We better find bandages"; Salem pierces her lips.

At that very moment I noticed the fire alarm ringing everywhere in each and every corner of the house.

"And a really huge hose to put off that fire"; I looked above the stairs in the direction of the cologne room.

Vixxi – 11

"Buildings! Buildings over buildings! Buildings ! buildings. Only after I came here did I realise that there is a sky too. Is that supposed to be sad? Is that supposed to be bad? I don't think so. I like buildings. But staying too much among them just gives me an ache. Same with the greens. The green air makes me puke after some time. That's why I like change. And more than change I like to see it happen. Like literally happen – like exposed out in the world like a change in feeling is a change in atmosphere, like a change in possibilities is a change in universe"; the authoress is looking out from the balcony railing; she feels princely. A womyn godly and majestic; her head high – bird-view high. She chuckles at her thoughts and say; "if only there were a balcony to make a balcony railing"; and there she goes back to writing.
No wonder they say drama is her last name!

Episode 28: Salem

"If am being honest, this would have had eventually happened to your skin with that many frequent tans and that many injections and pills"; I am trying to console Will, as I wrap his chest and thighs with bandages. He narrows his eyes. He doesn't seem consoled.

"On the bright side, the fire didn't burn your face and well wherever it burnt, it will just leave some scars that can be perfectly hidden by some clothes and makeup or surgery? I guess"; I try again. He grimaces. Well that's the best consolation I can come up with. What does he expect from me? Promise him a fairy godmother to show up and reverse time?

"I don't understand why am I not in the hospital"; this guy asks a lot of questions.

"It is because, we can't afford it"; I smile; he gives me an 'I-don't-believe-shit' look.

"What? Seriously"; I try to sound as believable as possible. I am in no condition risking my plan just for some pizza delivery guy's life.

"It's because, I am out of cash"; I smile to assure him. But he doesn't buy shit.

"You an Enoch is telling me that you are out of money?" he sounds unconvinced.

I give a bit of toothy grin as I say; "Unbelievable, right?" I tighten the bandages. Where in the hell did this Orleans go? First he screws up my plan and now he's vanished. Great idea getting him along in this plan Salem! Great idea!

"What in the hell's name is this cell supposed to do?" Speak of the devil and the devil appears.

I turn around and look at my burner phone in Orleans hand with some papers in his other hand.

"And you've got to explain me about these letters"; he presses on.

"Can you please drop those letters"; I roll my eyes in irritation. This is the very reason why people should not snoop into other people's lives.

"Actually, I cannot"; these letters have the same text written as the text messages in this 1947 dated cell phone"; Orleans looks at the phone with disgust. My forehead creases in confusion; "You do realise that cell phones never existed in 1947; in fact they are an invention of two decades ago"; it feels like am transferring him valuable knowledge.
He rolls his eyes on me. I give him a deadpan stare. "You know what I mean"; he pauses before he resumes pressing on me to tell what are the texts and the letters really about.
"They are very personal letters"; I move forward and drop the bandage on Will's chest, he cries in pain. "OUCH! Would you mind! Am in agony here"; I ignore Will and extend my hands to grab those letters and my burner phone.
Orleans backs away; "Uhuhh! Not gonna give it back to you until you tell me what do they mean"; he is dancing around the fire. I stomp and press my lips hard in frustration.
"Fine!"
 "You remember Amanda?" I gulp and take a deep breath before I move forward with this.
"Yea, the fake lover you are impersonating"; Orleans shrugs and after a second his eyes widen. "Don't tell me that Amanda writes such dirty talk!" yea I should have known – am screwed.
"Well, that is the only way my dad seems to participate in any relationship"; that is very true.

"Are you telling me that you've been writing dirty stuff to your dad"; for some reason Orleans dows not seem disgusted, for some reason there is a glittery gleam in his eye and a chuckle hidden in his voice. He finds this amusing. Great!

Of course he finds this amusing. The whole thing is like an entertainment channel 101.

Orleans looks inside the stupid burner phone and scrolls down the texts with a button; "Gawd! This is like the spiciest kind of incest gossip in my hands"; Orleans has a big mouth, I can bet he doesn't even realise that he is talking his thoughts out.

"Ohmygawd! Tie me to a chain!" he looks up at me with a naughty glance. I roll my eyes.

"Do you have hots for your dad?" great! now the great blabbermouth also knows about my secret agenda. I turn around to answer Will's question.

"Oh believe me Will should've seen her tape her mom, you'd say she has hots for her mother too"; Orleans suddenly realises he said too much.

"What?" Will's voice comes alarmed and risen, his eyes move back and forth from Orleans to me.

"Oops?" Orleans squeals.

Urgh! Am playing with four year olds here. I growl in desperate frustration.

"Shouldn't you be in pain?" I narrow my eyes. His forehead creases. I slap his bandaged chest, and he cries in pure agony. I take five folds of bandage and stuff his open mouth with it, muffling his agonising cry. Take some more of it and plug his ears with it. Now with firewall physically enabled in Will's physical software, I turn to face a very engrossed Orleans.

"OHMYFUCKINGGAWD!" he exclaims. There is nothing more I wish right now than killing this stupid asshole right here, right now.
I bite the insides of my cheeks. This guy is exhausting as he is dramatic.
Fine. If he likes exhausting then I like exhausting too. I'm gonna drain him till he breaks into pieces.

Episode 29: Orleans

I can't comprehend the amount of excruciating courage or should I say madness is needed to compose sexually inclined text messages and send them to your father as your father's new sexual interest. I mean wow. That must take a hella lot of guts and madness.
The following are proper evidences of a ruined mind, carefully developed by parents who like emotionally, sexually and individually suppressed children; children that are true forms of their extended fancy and not independent entities.

* * *

2:30 a.m.
A: Hey, Amanda
Amanda: Hey Mr. Adam
A: Guess where am I?
Amanda: where, Mr. Adam? ;*
A: Somewhere where am all wet and drenched. XXX
Amanda: Oooo! I guess I know that somwhere ;*

* * *

I couldn't read further than that.

"How were you even able to compose these terrifying lines into text messages?" I, by birth, am a curious person, I like to know the answer and not remain in the grey area.

Salem laughs as she rolls more bandage tape around Will's chest.

"Oh, you're so naive!" Nobody has ever called me naive. I blush in embarrassment.

"A girl in these days has to know her talks, irrelevant of who's on the other side. Text messages are the safest place for a girl to show her sexual self, a place where the screen becomes the mirror into the fantasy world. The whole thing has got nothing to do the fact with whom am I talking to. And moreover, mother and father has always preferred me no talking to boys outside family." Salem pauses, smiles and looks at me through the mirror and continues;

"See, am such an obedient girl but sadly my parents never respected that"; a frown replaces the smile.

I am astounded and completely in utter bewilderment (like I've been almost for the whole evening). As I have said before, and am gonna say again, nobody is as interesting as Salem; nobody can even possibly be Salem. That control, that power, that brain, that everything she has; all shout genius fornicating with madness.

"Mmm - mmm -mmm"; Salem taped him too, considering the amount he was screaming out of pain. 'It is all in good intention'; that's what she said when took out the bandage out of his mouth and put a duct tape over his lips.

"Must say, she must be really into BDS&M. First she talks about it with her father, tapes her mother and now poor Will! Hmm – she must be really into porn; either that or she just read fifty shades of grey way too many times to think BDS&M is cute.

"So, as I was telling you. I am being Amanda just so that I can get mother mad at father; not because I really want father to cheat. Me being Amanda ensures that he is not cheating. Do you get it?" she raises her forehead. What kind of perverted-twisted logic is that?

"Umm – actually Salem. I do not"; I pause to make it dramatic. Fuck hell, I woden my eyes wider to make her physically realise how insane does her logic sound. "Your father is unaware of the fact that there is no Amanda in existence. He must have tried tracing you back and forth even texting you. That suggests your father believes that Amanda that is you"; she nods like I am stating a fact; "is very much a real person"; I continue; "Hence, he is cheating on you"; I feel like am in the middle of proving an algebra statement.

"No – not technically"; she narrows her eyes. Will's eyebrows wiggle in agreement with me. See! Even the steroid-head pizza delivery guy understands the logic. "You see; I. AM. AMANDA"; she mouths her words as if am a ten month year old kid trying to understand words.

"So technically, my father isn't cheating" she presses her lips and slightly nods. I can't believe she's a genius idiot.

"You know what, you are right! He isn't cheating at all"; I repeat what she wish to mean; she smiles thinking that I agree with her.

"He is fucking doing incest. And you are fucking encouraging it"; I clench my teeth together. She slaps her forehead. Oh Gawsh! I can't even have a single sane conversation with this stupid-stupid-stupid yet incredibly manipulative genius.

"You are taking this so wrong!" she is defending her father. Does she realise how mad this looks? A minute ago, she was talking all about snatching away her father's property and now she's insanely protective of her father's moral authenticity.

Either she's fucking lunatic or she's fucking playing with me.

"This isn't incest. He doesn't know that Amanda is me or I am Amanda. He is just a corporate guy looking for some adventure and stress release which Amanda – not I that is Salem – is helping him give him"; she says. She's a fucking schizophrenic.

Will tilts his head with his eyebrows all stitched together. He is as lost with Salem's logic as I.

"Oh fucking Satan's mother! What did they make you eat when you were born? A battery 'cause you have potential apart logic. Sometimes you are at negative IQ level and sometimes you're shooting for infinity"; I wanna rip apart these dirty letters and choke her to death.

"I partly agree"; Salem smiles and looks at Will, who sheds her a deadpan stare.

"I am just doing what is needed to be done"; she looks at me with a toothy grin; "I am helping my family move forward and discard what is obsolete even if the obsolete means themselves. In the very means I might have made these obsolete assets look immoral but that does not count for these obsolete assets to be immoral at all. After all, it's all for the greater good"; she blinks way too many times.

"Oh now you're becoming a utilitarian! Shut the hell up; you are the most selfish person I know. Last one to be on this planet to be a utilitarian"; I snap. I am literally exhausted. She is killing me.

"On the contrary; my individual benefit is advantageous for this utilitarian purpose. And as we all know both these concepts are very deceptive and subjective. I am just honest. Transparent, as some would say. I believe in my principles as this family's. What is good for me, is good for my family. And that is what you should know"; she is babbling now.

"I don't get shit"; I frown on her logic. AGAIN.

"Oh I'll tell you shit!" she suddenly stands up gives me a smiley-creepy-little threatening stare; "Those letters; I composed to fucking ruin my parents and see how sleazy their ass is by my very self. I did all so because my parents have trained me to do one and only one thing. You know what that is? Fucking kill everyone that is in your way to success. They were. They wanted me cunning, they got me cunning. Those messages will be my insurance to my throne"; suddenly she isn't illogical.

"Showing them to my father would give me a direct ticket to my seat"; she pauses presses her lips, blows a bit of air out of the corner of her mouth making a string of her hair fly away; "And also I got a little bored. Wanted to see my father at his most vulnerable. Guess what? He's a walking gimmick"; she laughs and walks to the refrigerator.

"And yeah! I was just playing with you. My father is a fuck cheat and you are a melodramatic exhausting machine. So keep your mouth shut! Or see how I exhaust your engines out!" she takes out a champagne bottle and drinks directly from it.

What. A. Fucking. Bitch!

Episode 30: Salem

Dear Lord! This is soooo annoying! Where has mother kept all the open wine?!

"So that's what actually happened here"; Will and Orleans are bonding. Great! the pizza babe and the fashionhitler.

I didn't want him to know about Amanda. Like who the fuck he is to know about my plan? A helping hand doesn't qualify for a best friend – not even if he ends up as a partner in crime for life. I roll my eyes at the two idiots and open the drawer.

Oh! I found the cork opener. *Good!* Now atleast I can taste good old corked wine. I lick my lips in delight.

Episode 31: Orleans

Ping!

Oooo! I've got a new update on the new manga 'Daring Lovers'; the boys in it are super adorable. More like a story that I envy – more like a story that I fantasize. So, in this manga; there are like two guys; one is a vampire and the other is a werewolf. And as the myth goes (and the cliché) both the species are rivals. Saden; the werewolf guy takes Aspien; the vampire guy as a hostage. Saden is the prince of Laquo while Aspien is the prince of Vaxia. In an unexpected (totally expected) twist and turns they both find themselves in love with each other. But their love is forbidden! The question remains for the readers; will Saden and Aspien end up with each other and have a happily ever after or will they become the world's greatest tragedy?

It's a beautiful lovestory; with delicious layers to extreme sex.

Ring! Ring!

I look up from my phone and realise I've entered Salem's room. Heh! What a short trip! Expected a longer one taking the size of this mansion in account. Was it fidgeting that I saw that in the chair.

I pin my eyes to the chair for several minutes.

Yes! Yes it is!

Shit! Shit! What am I supposed to do now? I start panicking. Ms. Enoch is waking up; what am I supposed to do? My forehead is excreting sweat beads. I slowly step near, trying real hard to not step a creaking wood.

"You see that tree"; I stiffen at her voice. I look around just to check if there was someone else in the room. Nobody was there; she was the sole source of words.

My mind quickly orders my feet to turn a 180 degree turn and leave for Salem to tell her that Ms. Enoch has come to conscious and has taken off her mouth tape.
"Under that very tree Adam used to come...";
But something stops me from moving.
"Poor Adam used to come crying. Desperate in search for love"; Ms. Enoch continues, she smirks.
She sighs, I move forward. Out there in the big open balcony I step to behold the starlit panorama.
"I used to console him. Aahh! Those innocent times"; she takes a long pause.
"He used to call me his fairy godmother. Funny thing, I still am a fairy godmother to him. Not his wife"; she chuckles; "Damn! Now that I look back, I might have never ever been his lover as well. I was always his safe place. His fairy godmother"
The canopy of the tree was almost touching the balcony. The moon shone above. The stars were spread like sprinkled pixie dust. The owls were hooting somewhere. Somewhere close.
"But I disagree. There was something exceptionally magical when Adam had kissed me that morning. We were just seventeen, and I knew I loved him more than anything in the world. Or atleast I wanted him to be solely belong to me. I always wished him to be mine. He knows that. He knows that because he feels the same for me. But Adam isn't easy. Living with him is completely different from loving him. So different form saving him and consoling. Living with him is like – like – like forgetting yourself"; she takes another long pause.

I look at her. This feels wrong. So wrong. Her tears roll down her cheek. She is still looking at the big old tree in front of the open balcony. I can see two yellow eyes looking at us through the veil of leaves. *Oh, there's the owl!* I spot him.

An unusual creature of the night.

"But – but – but you know what? It's impossible. If you knew me you'd know I don't compromise myself for the sake of others. A trait I developed long ago as a child. A virtue on which my integrity is built on. It frustrated me in the beginning – started gnawing me, and then came Salem. And as much as I wished her to become my refuge – Oh Darling! – the world knows she became my life's biggest regret"; she sniffed.

Her eyes stuck on the tree; her mind somewhere far away in a universe unknown to me, her eyes pondering into somewhere infinite. She wasn't talking to me.

"Nothing like a girl child. Nothing like me. She was as much covered in alien genes inside as she was on outside. Except her face"; she pauses; "Her face somehow managed to stay in the family. But soon even that lost its charm. She is arrogant, indolent, ungrateful and most undesirable. All I ever wished was to bear a child sweet as honey, sharp as a knife, clever as a fox and adaptive as a female. But what I got a reckless, crying, yelling, obstinate as stone child"; her eyebrows stitched together in anger.

"You say a child never had the choice to come in this world. I say neither did I have the choice to bring a child of my own – bloody – desires"; her eyes back from the infinity looks straight at me.

"That's bloody unfair of you to say so"; I whisper.

"Unfair?" her voices raises high enough to make my heart squirm but not enough to leave the room and warn Salem.

"You know what is unfair? Unfair is being told to have never spoken. Unfair is being beaten half to death. Unfair is conceding to those beliefs and notions that you never believed in just so you could survive. Unfair is losing your entire identity while converging into someone else's unfair is doing it happily with full consent 'cause you're not aware of the otherwise – well either that or you're too afraid to be aware of it. Unfair, you say? Unfair? Oh you poor priviledged dummies – you don't even know half the meaning of what you say. You don't – you don't..."; she starts mumbling.

I don't like this. I mean I feel sorry for her and all but why is she saying that we or worse I don't know what unfair is! I mean I feel shit just clarifying people to people that I am gay. That I like boys. I like it and I hate that I can't feel normal about it even when it is normal around me.

"Stop"; words just leave my mouth and I don't know why. Atleast Ms. Enoch stopped with her mumbling. "Stop – please stop"; she is looking at me. "I feel like shit. I feel like fucking shit to have done you this or even had Salem tie you up"; I meet her gaze. She doesn't seem to be moved or even disappointed by my words.

"I come from a really low family background. My mother, she has a local downtown salon; my father, he's employed himself as a basic violent drunkard. I have no shot at living a rich, luxurious life. Fortunately enough, unlike all the other children in my neighbourhood, my parents did not force me into quitting my education and support them with finance. And the worst part is that – 1"; I squeeze my eyes and press my fingers against my side veins. "The worst part is that my hormones do not even act normal... they don't act normally at all. And I know am gonna break my heart when they do realise who I am – what I am!" I can feel my rage rise; " I can't even complain them of being homophobic much less ever accuse them of it. I can't – I just can't. 'Cause am relatively priviledged but not priviledged enough and this 0 this enough part it gnaws me – it takes away my calm makes me angry and so angry and feel so unfair. So tell me Ms. Enoch... tell me how is that I do not get the right to feel unfair?" I don't realise that am looking at the hooting owl on the tree. I turn around after a couple of minutes of silence. "Great!"

Now I am a certified fool. The chair is occupied by her diamond necklace; and the shreds of tape all torn by the stone.

Shit!

She's gone. Of course she's gone. I am so fucking crazy dumb. I close my eyes and use my magical powers to detect Ms. Enoch's presence.

Huh?!

I open my eyes. My magic shows that she's here. I enter Salem's room; switch on the lights and call her name out. I ardently beg Ms. Enoch to never leave Salem's room. I call her name out again and again. I check Salem's closet, her washroom, I check the balcony again. I check the space behind the bedpost, the space under the bed.

"Ms. Enoch?" I call, my eyes alert to spot her.

"Why are you looking for my mother under the bed?" That is definitely Salem I hear at the door. I turn my head to look at her.

"Uh-oh!" I squeeze my eyes and press my lips waiting in anticipation for her to freak out on realising that we lost her mother.

Okay fine!

I lost her mother.

Vixxi - 12

We humans are so gullible that we'd rather understand the concept of a dream than reality.
Dreams are the only memory romantic enough, to make us gullible enough to believe in them. And that sort of gullibility and romanticisation is what we should all preciously preserve for ourselves.
So what are we; gullible or romantic?

Episode 32: Salem

"What did you do, Orleans?"
Infront of me is an empty chair with my tapes all torn and no sign of my dear ol' mother.
I turn around expecting to see a scared face but a laughing asshole is what I meet.
"Gawd - you sucked the fun out with all that taping"; he has the audacity to defend himself. How dare he!
"Did you feel pity?" I narrow my eyes.
Orleans laugh stops, and tries to steal away his eyes.
"Of course you did! You are all about - oh! She's a mother for Gawd's sake. She deserves a second chance - fucking human rights have killed rational neurons these days. Fuck! Fuck! Fuck them!" I yell at him.
"Look at me Orleans! Isn't it so?" I grit my teeth and repeat.
"Don't sneak your eyes away! DON'T."
But he doesn't listen.
"Well -"; he mutters to himself.
Of course, the drama king himself melt out in front of my mother's puppy crying eyes.

"Well – what?" I snap.

"Don't snub me!" he replies back sharply.

"You know Orleans; you are not so much of a sharp brain as much as you are a sharp tongue";

"I highly doubt if that flimsy opinion would matter to me";

"Oh, it should. It should 'cause I swear to your fucking Lucifer that I'll kill you if she leaves this fucking house"; I narrow my eyes to the point that can I feel my eyelashes meet.

Orleans reddens.

"What were you thinking?" I yell again check out the sad remains of my perfectly planned out plan.

"Well for starters, I thought she'd had enough"

"Oh – ohkay"; - I tauntingly nod my head in mocking seriousness.

"That is so considerate"; I grind my teeth harder.

Orleans gives me a deadpan look.

"Well – then I saw tears running down her face and –"

"– and?" I tilt my head – I know what must have had happened.

"Well she was kinda right"; Orleans murmurs in the back.

"Kinda right?" I raise my voice.

"Oh I'll tell you! She must have definitely used how her struggle is nothing compared to what we struggle. Kill me if she hadn't mentioned how you are lucky to acknowledge your individuality rather meeting up with someone's else's bar of expectations"; I glare Orleans, he gasps and his eyes widen.

"How did you know?" he asks.

"She is my fucking mother. I know her inside out. I have no friends. What do you think I do? Analysing and deconstructing my family's psyche is rather more of my job than this family's therapist"; he deserves my loud voice.

"Oh! How am I suppose to ignore a perfectly doe-eyed person who was crying a river"; he stomps his feet like a little child unable to vocalise his thoughts so steals away to adhere to tantrums.

"What happened next?" I come straight to the point.

"Well one thing lead to another and then I freed her from bondages but only after when she promised me to follow me to you"; he widens his eyes to strengthen his defence suit.

"Oh! Of course she promised and of course you are dumb enough to believe her. Thank your mother that you have magic otherwise you'd be in worse conditions than a child below poverty line in a developing country";

"Oh please!" he is finally offended – that sweet piece of rhinoceros guilt guard.

"Seriously! Have you met yourself? Calling me a rhinoceros guilt guard? You are the biggest rhino guilt guard – hell! You are a rhino guilt WALL!" He yells and spits on my face.

"I take a pause, my expressions are a mix of disgust and grimace. I clean my face with my hands.

Huh! Wait! What's that?

"Is that music playing?" Orleans hears it too. His eyebrow wiggle in a question mark and his eyes are busy guessing the tune.

Goosebumps creep on my skin. I know what's happening. Suddenly my body temperature rises and I guess the song.

"What happened next Orleans? She didn't follow you did she?" I ask him; his eyes come sneaking back from the song to me.

"Well I thought she was following me until I turned around just before leaving the room and she had disappeared. I checked everywhere in the room but she wasn't here. So, I thought of giving my magic GPS a shot and – a funny thing happened"; he chuckles to himself. I can feel the lyrics come to me.

This is my favourite song. I look away from him to the door.

"What funny thing?" I repeat.

"She was here – right here somewhere in the room – unreachable – and that is impossible, right – right?" his little chuckles vanishes. I step out of the balcony.

"Great goodness"; I mumble to myself.

I run out of the room.

This song – this song makes me feel drugged. Like am on the beach, on a haunted, haunted beach. I hate loving this song.

I stop at the railing and look down. It's going to be a battle; I can predict; Aeolus v/s Apollo. I am Apollo, of course.

One must be wondering;

Playlist? Why would a sane person who was just taped to a chair play her playlist instead of calling the police or better running away.

Well – Enoch likes to dead with each other themselves rather taking help.

And playlists – playlists is their hunt call.

Each of our playlist is our secret diary. It is that secret diary that we play before stabbing each other to a litany of condescending insults or – death.

Last time a hunt call was made it was basically on my grandmother's funeral. Or I happen to also call it my father's coronation day. He played the playlist right under her stinking rotting dead nose.

My Gama was the most intelligent person I've ever known. And also perhaps the only person I ever trusted. After her death, nothing seems to come close to me. Doctor said she died because of her fat; I say she died because of dad.

My Gama was many things; she was a single parent, widow and a CEO but she wasn't a great human. Killing her was the easiest thing that my dad had to do. It was easier than getting married to my mother even. Poor Gama! Didn't see all those omega-6 components in her green veggies coming.

We weren't even able to give her a proper funeral; with all the new CEO duties piling up on dad's desk, it became hard for the family to soak in the tragedy. So father decided to better sell the precious body to science or as my father so eloquently said:

"She can fucking have my dick than a funeral".

I literally hate-hate-hate loving this song.

"Is that?" Orleans voice brings me back to the present. To the mystical music creeping down my spine and reviving my childhood memories.

All curled up in clothing suitcase with my mother tearing up in the corner sipping to wine and whining to one of her sisters about how she is nothing but a mere puppet to her husband.

Her times weren't as free as ours for women. Her times were all about revolutions; sadly, I don't relate to that. I just can't. I just can't imagine a world where Orleans is given more preference than me just on the basis of his genitals, well technically in that world Orleans won't be Orleans. He'd be some sad little dude with a girlfriend frustrated with life and his sexuality. Good for us, we didn't see this struggle, we are better as a generation, we skip the sad part of all obstructions and hurdles and put more energy to productivity. Ignorant or not, I hardly care. What I care is that I am not gonna drink wine, whine while packing. I will drink wine and whine while my assistant packs my luggage for me. Now, that's more like me. "Is that what I think it is"; Orlean's voice brings me back to the reality again. These playlists have so many rare impressions on my memeories that they all come flooding back.

"Is that..."; he guesses

But I interrupt and give his mouth the words they seek; "Hotel California by Eagles";

"Who played it?" he asks.

"Mother"; I reply, my jaw grinds tightly.

"Where is Will?" he leans over the railing to get a peek at Will but that's not possible.

"I can't see him; where is he?"he repeats again.

"Grounded";

I answer.

Vixxi – 13

Has someone ever wondered that we all are born and trapped in a gravty twilight loop. We all go round and round and round the sun and relatively round and round and round the centre of the galaxy.
But we have tricked ourselves into escaping it; we have evolved in ourselves psychologically perceive linear flow of time and yet pocket memories that have the potential to destroy us or to help us move on.

Episode 33: Orleans

Grounded? More like under-grounded.
"How is that as we go deeper down this wine cellar the light lamps go dimmer?" I ask as I lift my flashlight.
"Don't know, mother likes the aesthetics of an authentic-dungeon dungeon"; Salem says, she moves forward down the spiralling dungeon alley.
"If that's so, why does it smell garden here?" this place really does smell wonders, if I hadn't known it being a dungeon, I might as well make it my hideout home.
"Have we not had had a discussion on my mother and her cologne obsession"; she answers.
"Oh yeah! Think we burned that conversation soon"; I shrug and snicker at my humour, but she didn't find it that funny since she gives me a death glare the second that joke makes it out of my mouth.
"Couldn't you use your magic and just tell me wherever my mother is?" she barks at me.

"I will not use my dearest magic. I have made that sufficiently clear"; I am repeating that constantly and I will repeat the same answer again and again.

"Atleast tell me why so that I'd stop thinking you less of a burden who needs to be murdered and more of an accomplice"; she steps down the stairs of the stony dungeon. It is getting down here. Everything smells like a rose blooming in some corner, but when you reach that corner, a very green chlorophyll rich moss is seen growing under the dripping water which I hope does not belong to the sewage pipe.

"The reason is clear. Do you not know it?" I say as I try my best straying away from the dirty walls. My eyes are on a death alert. A single touch could ruin my whole outfit forever. And I just had a changeover.

"Heeello! Do I look like I belong to a witchcraft-goth-obsessed cult?" her high-pitched tone gets on my nerves.

"Don't know, looking at your mother's magic-slash-witchcraft obsession hard to tell that you either belong to that cult or are starting one of your own"; I bark back. Salem gives me a side-glare and gives a look to the wall for a slight second. I catch her thoughts through her eyes and readily jump to my rescue in no second; "Don't you dare think of shoving me against that wall. This outfit. It will tear into pieces and also I'd be leaving you with a totally healthy memory rich mother"; I don't even know why Salem tries thinking otherwise.

She rolls her eyes; "Well, the thought was worth the shot"; she shrugs, smiles and narrows her eyes; "Interestingly"; she steps forward toward me; "you are not residing to your go-to magic witch-y abilities at all. Now it strikes me to dig deeper as to why aren't you using your magic at all here? Tell me Orleans, why aren't you?" Salem steps is standing right under my nose, giving me the U-V rays sun glare herself.
I pout; fuck it! Nothing like an FBI classified information anyway!
"I can't use magic more than once in the dungeons"; there I said it all out and loud. Salem takes a minute to take it all in. And after that minute, she's ROTFLOL. Great! Now I have literally hired a person to laugh at me on my face.
"You may think that that is funny, but it's not. Especially not for the cauldron folks –"; I try to complete the clarification but then she pin points again;
"OHMAGAWD! YOU CALL YOURSELF CAULDRON FOLKS!" and in a moment she's slapping the floor out of laughter. Such modesty – ah! I wonder why doesn't it die out sooner!
"Yea laugh it all away. But us warlocks and witches, we are just cursed like that. Dungeons ain't our air to breathe in. We like it lavish and big, luxurious and air-conditioned. Dungeons and slaughterhouses make us go craaazy"; I go off about this whole laugh-out-loud situation. With my words reaching to Salem's ear, she suddenly stops, her laugh turns into a snicker, a lip tight snicker.

"Oh! In that case; you have just entered your warlock nightmare"; her lip-tight snicker devilishly breaks into horrific words.

"What do you mean?" I can feel my forehead cringe and my spine come to cautious alert.

"This is not just a dungeon. Over her is the chicken slaughter haunted house that I've constructed for the next Halloween"; Salem tries stifling her smile, but her nefarious muscles fail to accomplish that.

"What?" I am not afraid of a chicken slaughter haunted house. Haunted house are for kids.

Well yes, I wanted something different this time, the bad thing is Halloween is two days away. But the good thing is the haunted house is working"; she chuckles.

What I am afraid of is an Enoch chicken slaughter haunted house and their sincere drive to achieve authenticity.

Episode 34: Salem

"Not in even fucking hell's wrath am entering that"; Orleans just can't wait to show tantrums.

I scoff at his persistent childish fits. "Cummon! Aren't you a darn witch? You should feel darkness like home or something"; I sluggishly say.

Orleans gives me an eye and before he even starts I know his words; "That is so stereotyping of you!" he narrows his eyes and continues distracting the actual point that needs to be given consideration; "It's like saying every woman is beautiful"

"huh?" I am lost here, isn't every woman beautiful?

"Or like saying every man is the head of the family. All this shit conforms us to believe into certain traits. We aren't fucking Java programms, being made into objects with specific traits";
"That or we are fucking Java programms with just a more complex and instantaneous communicatory abilities within ourselves as well as outside ourselves"; I raise my eyebrow. I will tear this guy apart if he doesn't stop talking.
"And maybe that's why we adhere to manipulation"; I put my hand around Orlean's shoulder back, I look at him as he looks deeper into the darkness of the dungeon from the opening. The stairs lead directly into the serpentine alleys of the dungeon.
"What do you mean?" He looks away from the darkness and rest his eyes at me. I smile at him produce my right hand; "Like my beautiful ring"; I profusely give a toothy smile at my ring; the blue diamond on the silver band sparkles as it refracts the escaping light of the wine cellar bulbs.
It catches Orleans gaze just in time for him to see the ring slide of my finger (with a slight help of my thumbs) (okay! A lot of help of my thumbs) and drop in the air followed by a (intentionally given) bounce by my hand, followed by my yell;
"OHHHHHH NOOOOOO! MY RIIIIIIEENNGG!"

Followed by (as expected) Orleans sudden reflex of reaching out to catch the ring, followed by his feet slipping on the platform step, followed by him taking a flight in the air, followed by him dropping down the stair of the dungeon, followed by me shutting the wine cellar closed, followed by a loud noisy vanishing cadence of crash and thud and crash and thud and crash until finally the last thud brings a bone-cracking stop to the series of these unfortunate events.
"Oops?"
Whatever, I got my work done and that's what matters.

Episode 35: Orleans

A question, if we move in the opposite direction of the earth's rotation do we exert more force than when we move in the same?
Or is that just a stupid question made by someone who was stupid enough to not make use of google and rather let her foolish pursuits ignore the other factors required in asking this question. For instance: Theory of relativity that just might negate the effect of earth's rotation on human limb movement on account of its micro level.
Or is it's just that I am babbling inside my head because I just exploded like a nebula.
NEBULAHHHH!! I can see the sparks in the black void.

Or is that void? What if it's some kind of matter with a different fundamental chemical composition. They call it the black matter; what if the vacuum is just vacuum for the white matter for hence it can be matter for black matter. I wonder what composes this black matter? Hmmmmmm...

I surely have hit my head hard. My inner conscious shakes his head and makes a raspberry to clear my thoughts.

My eyes slit open.

I wasn't wrong. The earth *is* moving against me. I can feel it in my hips.

"Oh wake up already, you fat piece of lump. I can't drag you all the way down here"; my ears beg to go back to the sounds of nebula bursting and my subconscious chattering in gibberish. I can't disagree with them, listening to Salem is like listening to a viper talk; constantly in want of biting someone to death.

My blurry vision clears and I realise that the earth is still and it is me who is being dragged callously down this piss-smelling, moss-growing, ancient path.

"Drop my leg"; the memories come to me rushing like a Japanese train (wait! Wouldn't that be slow for a brain? Nevermind, it's just a metaphor) and they aren't pleasant. The fall was like hitting the Japanese train again and again.

"Stop dragging ME! And fucking drop my leg"; the snobbish brat just doesn't realise the meaning of my said words.

"Stop shouting at me!" she half-opens her mouth as if astonished at being talked so rude; as it were I who been a burden to her and she had in her kind gesture dragged me around. WOW! Great depiction, Salem. Great depiction!

"What do you mean by 'stop shouting at me?'and when are you thinking about dropping that leg of mine, huh?" I look at her with wide-baffled eyes, sometimes am thankful she had Ms. Enoch as a mother. A bitch deserves a bitch.

"Sorry"; she scoffs silently, rolls her eyes and just like that drops my leg under the influence of gravity.

"Ouch! – not like that. My nerve receptors are still busy processing what kinda anti-crash protocol they have to take. Thanks to you"; my eyes narrow on cue.

"Oh it's my pleasure, finally your motor cells are at work otherwise I thought they had completely lost themselves to your extra expressive face – which is so annoying!" believe right now it's her face that's begging for a punch.

"Fuck you"; I ignore her. The bitch is a psychopath and on top of that thinks that she's doing this all for the great cause for protecting her family legacy. Gawd! I fear what will happen to the poor priest whom, if ever, she confesses to.

"Urgh!!!"she wobbles her feet like a child throwing a tantrum; "Get up! Get up! GET UP!" as I said – a *child throwing a tantrum.* "If mother finds us here, I'll be doomed. She'll never stop making fun of me and how I walked in the dungeons in my nighties with a weird guy who probably she'll mention as my friend"; her forehead creased a thousand folds and her chin was in the air,

"The bitch!" I snap. "That's what you concerned about! Last I remember you don't fucking give a second thought when you posted that BDS&M pic of ours, huh?" I get up and stare at her with the most surprised face possible.

I. Am. Hurt.

She takes her tongue out, and lazily droop her eyelids and start mocking me speak; "Blah! Blah blah! Blah – unnnunn"; I don't know why but I grab her tongue and start mocking her.

"Mommy – mommy blah blah blah mommy daddy mommmy bladadada daddy blah blah blah. I hate mommy. Oh I love mommy. Mommy concerns me this. Oh mommy I love you Mommy mommy mommy sucha bish mommy gimme my sandles blah blah blah mommy mommy..." she narrows her eyes but I don't stop quitting mocking her ass off her.

"mommy dududu blah blah blah mommy mommy daddy – WTF!" suddenly something flashes past in between Salem and me; my neck jerks away in the direction of the flashing thing. Everything follows into a slow motion; a stinging sensation follows somewhere in my body.

My eyes deny inspecting into what gave me a sudden rush of pain.

They were adamant to recognise what past them. An escaping light struck the edge of the object and it sparkled, hinting it to be metal. Following them was a flying piece of pink – flesh? Is that flesh? I narrow my slits to focus and I see blood shooting out of the flesh's rear end, the blood twirling in air like ribbon in flight or like a ballerina in torque.

It's a finger! I realised.

Thud!
Bang!
A striking sound comes as the flying object hits the wall. My eyes recognise it. And panic as they have never panicked before.
A butcher's knife.
Great!
 As far as logic worked my eyes became well aware what had just happened. My head flips in the direction of the burning pain. My eyes met a pool of blood oozing out of my dear old finger and dripping down on the ground.
MY MIDDLE FINGER IS IN HALF!
It was no more holding a wobbling wet tongue. It was literally half; I look and without even realising realised that I'd been screaming since the first contact of the butcher's knife and my finger.
"THAT'S MY FUCKING FINGER!" I shout out at Salem and in a reflex take my shirt with the other finger and cover it. I am trying to stop the bleeding, but that's **IMPOSSIBLE** when you half your finger in bloody half. I look at Salem, with fiery anger and bloody vengeance burning in my eyes. Blood is splattered across her face like tiny dots of paint. Her eyes are droopy and she looks indifferent but disappointed.
"Now I'd have to wash my face. Thank you, Axel. Thank you very much"; she opens her bitch-fed mouth.

"WHAT? MY FUCKING FINGERING FINGER JUST CUTOFF AND YOU SAY THAT!" Tears roll down my cheek in pain, my shirt has gone all red, and this woman cares that she'd have to wash her face, again!

"Oh! Don't worry, you anyway have no need of a fingering finger. Boys like a grip of thumb"; she speaks so casually that it irritates me to the point that I wanna punch her. But I can't. My baby finger is detached from its mama hand.

Salem turns around and looks at someone. There – there stands the fucking murderer of my finger.

"Mother, please apologise before he starts with all his tantrums and burst of feelings and all those unnecessary emotions"; Salem's request looks more like a blatant statement that had once been roted and now has been vomited out. Ms. Enoch comes out in the light and I am left starstruck. I would have been more expressive but at the moment a more grave feeling reigned over my expressive face.

She is a perfect beauty. If God were a devil, she would look exactly like her. Poised, calm, tenacious, beautiful and most of all confident.

"It's not my fault Salem, his finger was in contact with your tongue. The same tongue that touches my silver cutlery. And you know how I like my cutlery – sterilised and hygienic; not – "; she pauses, looks at me, scrunches her nose and gives away a disgusting expression.

" – filthy and infected."

In my defense, she just cut my beautifully pedicured finger into half. If am not in distress and in filthy rich pain, am not a human. Apparently this logic – it doesn't settle with the Enochs much.

Vixxi – 14

The Grand Design.
Our world is fond of designs. We are fond of
fashioning our minds, societies, our resources, our
abilities, our lives and most importantly our closets.
Without design, nothing can ever be crafted.
Only a grand design could flourish alone.
A Grand design does not need to be right or wrong. It
does not need a witness to prove that it is grand. All
that a Grand Design needs is to make people buy it.

Episode 36: Salem

"What in the hell's name are you upto, huh?" my
mother's voice thunders down the dungeon. I can't lift
my head and confront her. She is scary.
"What were you trying to gain? This is absolute
nonsensical, because I am not getting at any reason as
to why was I knocked out and tied up like one of your
play dolls?" She hollers at me.
"I am sorry, I was just trying to execute a plan"; I pause
and take a peek at her; "You know, a plan that I'd
made so you could proudly say that I am your
daughter"; I try giving her my puppy eyes.
She blankly stares at me and speak after a minute;
"Last time you pulled off that horrid face, I suggested
you plastic surgery. Do you never care to listen to me?
You will repent this in future, you know when you are
all wrinkly and too old to avoid atrophy"; sometimes I
wonder how exactly I'll kill my mother.

Maybe I'll poison her, or maybe I'll suffocate her or better yet I'll just bribe the doctor and surgically change her botox morphology to a surgery gone wrong.

Hmmm... that would kill her.

Or should I just give her skull and face a laser hair removal treatment. I chuckle inside; now that's evil even for my standards.

"Stop smirking like an idiot"; she snaps at me. My eyes again droop down and stare at the floor.

"First you arrest me of my senses, then you allow entry of a homeless boy and a pizza guy –"; "Excuse me am not homeless"; Orleans defends himself in the background; he sounds whiny and timid. I subconsciously roll my eyes; he should be thankful that it was his finger and not my tongue that got cut off otherwise imagine the horror!

" – and on top of that you are walking around the mansion with only in your nighty on and don't even start me with your face and hair. What kind of a lady keeps herself that way?"

"Not a Victorian one for sure"; Orleans sarcastically comments. He's doomed.

"Hey, Finger boy"; mother calls him; "Next time I'll chop your tongue off along with those eyebrows of yours that constantly wiggle like earthworms shittin'"; that must have shut him up. Thankfully!

I do not take the risk of taking a sneak of Orlean's expression, but I amuse myself by wondering how abashed his face would be.

"And you little cute butt"; Shit! She'll know about Will.

"Why the hell are you delivering pizza to my house?" I can feel the wrath in her voice, and I can imagine the fury in her eyes. Junk food is banned in this house. According to the famous Enoch saying; *We sell fat, we never eat fat;* a perfect saying for a perfect junk food manufacturing corporation. Quite contrary to the catchphrase with which this corporation advertises its food; *Taste to die for!*
Or maybe not that contrary.
"I – I – I – "; Will whimpers to form a sentence.
"What I – I – I? Stop stuttering and speak with confidence"; her eyes must have had gone laser, poor Will, he will die down here.
"I am in pain. Stop shouting at me!" I can hear his tears roll down his face.
"What a whiny little creature you are!" she remains unsympathetic.
"And may I ask how you got burnt?"she asks with authority. My mother is really good with that voice.
"I have zero clue! One minute –"; my head jerks up. Oh he's going to get us all killed.
"Forget that I asked! I have no time to spare on your insignificant piece of information"; mother ignores him and I take a sigh of relief. She unlocks her phone and probably checks on her notifications.
Wait! The House Fire Alarm! It sends notifications to my parent's phone every time it activates.
My anticipate mother's eyebrows contorting as she goes through her screen. My eyes move to Orleans's; he is unaware of the future and so is Will who has started playing with his bandages.
"What in the hell's name!" I hear mother mumble – and there her eyebrows contort.

"Fuck!" The word escapes my lips even before I could prevent them.

"YOU SET FIRE IN MY COLOGNE ROOM?" her head jerks up as her glares turn into light sabers trying to stab me. She briskly walks towards me, her hands in aggression and absolute fury closed in a tight fist.

"Don't worry darling, I've already booked an appointment with my plastic surgeon for you"; she gives me a narrow slit evil-smile. Oh gawd my poor little face!

I brace myself for a punch. But luck had left my side since Orleans decided to stay on.

Bang!

A floating shoe hits my mother's skull and physically humiliates her dignity;

"Leave her alone!" Orleans shouts at my mother's back.

She clenches her teeth and turn half-way around. Her eyes furious and kindling hell fire.

She looks at Orleans and then stares at me. And now the question comes whom will mother murder with her bare hands? The murderer of her tastes a.k.a me or the murderer of her dignity a.k.a Orleans.

Obviously I knew the answer. Orleans stands straight in upright position with only one foot shoed and ready to run a marathon. Will is standing beside him. Neither of them knows what they have just done. My mother's dignity is far more precious to be played with – far far more precious. In simple words Orleans is dead.

"You dangling son of a BIIIIIITTTTCTCCCCCHHHHHHHHHHH!" oh damn she swore!

"Run. NOW! RUN!" I shout and try to get away when suddenly mother grabs me by the arm and stops me. Her hands tighten around my arm; I could feel her fingers thrusting against my bones.
"Lemme go!" I shout at her face, but she doesn't leave. Her eyes promise me hell.
BANG!
My heart skips a beat. Another shoe comes flying on my mother's face – hitting her exactly on her nose – hopefully flattening it!
"That's for my thumb bitch!"
Orleans shouts and without wasting time, I scoot my ass as far as possible and start running with lightening speed.

Vixxi-15

It's enigmatic how one suddenly wishes Time to be a physical entity; to touch it and hug it; to say I love this very moment and to feel it warmly covering oneself like a blanket in a wintery cold night.

Episode 37: Orleans

"Run. You have to run"; I shout at Will, who is following behind me.

"Duck!" Salem shouts from behind. As soon as I duck, a butcher knife passes over me and falls on the floor. I turn around the corner. Ms. Enoch kinda lost her mind about when Will opened his mouth and confided in her the 'accidental' blowing up of her cologne museum.

In Will's defence; Ms. Enoch can be more than intimidating – she can be terrifying!

"Run faster you piece of lump"; Salem shouts at Will. "I would, had I not been burnt by the magic boy"; he dare satirize. Strike down my defence for his defence. New defence: In my defence I didn't know my magic could be that strong that it would literally blow up the whole place just because I was feeling hot!

"You better quicken you steps pizza boy. Don't want my mother to chop your roasted meat too!" Salem's sweet sounding threat really helped in rushing Will's feet.

"You all are DEAD! Do you hear me DEAD. And you little Salem – you madam are grounded for life!" Ms. Enoch shouts behind our running feet.

"That's UNFAIR!" I shout back.

Another whisp of sound travels in the air warning us of a coming butcher knife.

"HOW DOES SHE HAVE A STORE SIZE SUPPLY OF BUTCHER KNIVES???!" Will yells beside me as his pace quickens.

"Thank the lords she doesn't have guns?!" I shout.

"THANK THE LORDS?! WHY WOULD I THANK THE LORDS ABOUT THAT! SHE IS ANYWAY GOING TO CHOP OFF US AND SELL US WITH THAT PIG MEAT SHE SELLS!"

"IN THAT CASE I'D SINCERELY LIKE TO BE SOLD AS PEPPERONI PIZZA"; Orleans shouts back, his comment had me laughing in no minute.

"What?" Will has been already craz-ied out enough for the night to understand the underlining sarcasm in that macabre.

"Why the fuck can't you use your goddamn magic, huh?" Salem gives me here blazing eyes. She is pissed at me for not using my magic. "All the fucking while you were protecting yourself with magic but down here when you *actually* are in need of your witch-crafty protection, your fingers are glued – GREAT!" she growls at me.

If it were not for my superstitious scare for losing magic in the dungeons, I'd had transported all of us outta here in a blink of an eye. But what can I say! As magic-folk lore goes, our breed died being burnt on stakes and slaughtered inside dungeons.

Down here – I'll save my spell like a 50's girl saves her virginity.

"Stop dishing at me! Had you not tied your mother in the first place, we would have not been running in these historically creepy dungeons. I mean – who even have dungeons in this century?!"
"Scottish people?" Will remarks in the background.
"Now why the fuck would you say that?!" I look back at him and quickly duck as I see another knife thrown our way. Ms. Enoch is certainly a super fast runner, she isn't even puffing yet.
"He's not completely wrong"; Salem lifts her cheek with a side smile shrug.
"Not kiddin' – I heard that there were these big house castles where the dungeons were still running or something"; Will tries to substantiate his argument.
I won't be surprised if my face would be radiating a *weirded-out* look rather a *freaked-out* at the moment; "Great time to throw in your fallacious generalised opinion. And if you are done, can we please come back to saving our lives"; staying with this group, I, indefinitely feel the most logical and probably the most normal person. And if am the most pragmatic and normal person around, there is seriously something wrong.
"You are such a boring a-hole"; Salem's voice is inhumanly in its normal tempo.
"Thank – uh fu – huh – li"; my words take breaks as I try to inhale as my oxygen possibly available in this underground labyrinth.
"Run after me – I'll take you to a hidden room behind the slaughter trash bin"; Salem orders casually.
But I am disgusted from inside.
How does this place still smells like roses when there is a slaughter trash bin stored inside!

I swear, sometimes it does feel like money is magic.

Episode 38: Salem

I know the feeling. I know the feeling too well. The fuck she decided to distort my face! Urghhhh!!! Am so crazy mad at her right now. I wanna chop her to little little pieces. But I wanna love her too. For a moment she was almost so proud of me on learning my plans. It made me wanted to throw a party for her – to hug her. Fuck I wanted to show her love like no man ever could. I wanna treat her like a queen. Maybe just to gain a selfish favour out of it. But yes I wanna treat her like a queen. And I wanna fight. Yes I wanna fight. But I'm not supposed to. I can't. Oh! Fuck with my plan – how the hell did she even get conscious?! But right now am so mad at her – I wanna just smack her for thinking to smack me right in the face. But I can't. Shit! I can't. Not until she's asleep. Not until she's unconscious. Not until I am gaurenteed that she won't remember a bit of all that I did. Because when she's awake. Am not allowed to revolt. Am not allowed to be disobeyed. Am forbidden from my feelings. Calling them naive and hormonal. Because that is what I am. Naive and hormonal. And maybe she will forgive me. Shouldn't she? Isn't this all the part of naive and hormonal excuse? Isn't this supposed to be my biology.
The blurry vision of the flames comes to focus, as we hide in the storage room behind the chicken waste bins. It reeks roses here.
Orleans is right, How is that even possible!

"Do you think that the reason why robots can't ever become humans is the speck of star dust constellated in us?" Will asks.

"That's what you worried about right now?" he replies "Answer me"; he insists.

"Yea. Am no scientist but that could be the single most ingredient that could explain the electricity running through us and still not frying us to roasts"; he, for some reason, replies like an even more insane person than he already is.

 "That's stupid"; I gently mutter. My eyes never leave the burning flames.

"Why?" I can hear Will ask.

"Robots are also made of stardust. It's in their substance matter dumbasses. Everything on earth has specks of stardust. Just because you believe the animate to be superior to inanimate does not vanish the fact that inanimate too is made of stardust. And robots don't need some fucking stardust to make them humans, they need good programming"; by the end of my sentence, my words start to feel like little coughs of scoffs.

There is a pause before he breaks it; "I liked – I liked the way you said 'constellated in us'. It feels as if we are living constellations after all"; Orleans smiles. I chuckle away at his apprentice-like appreciation.

"But I must give you that; robots are much better off without being like humans, so star dust or not, it hardly matters"; he is a born romantic, can't end the conversation with a cold shoulder.

"Yea; with a human, everything becomes so this and that. With robots, things are clear. It's all about input, processing and output. I mean a robot would understand what am doing with my mother, right?" I play along for amusement.
"Would understand or wouldn't care to understand the reason to understand at all"; he raises his eyes.
I scoff and roll my eyes; "Whatever! I hardly care"; I look forward deeper into the dungeon trying to get a glimpse of what is beyond the illumination of the bright flames.
"I have a very contrary opinion on that. I love the spice and drama in the processing. I mean isn't it the third thermodynamics law?" Orleans takes my attention.
"Like pizza"; Will interposes in the background.
"What do you mean?" I ask.
"I mean, regardless of being human or not, isn't the input we give always more than the output. Machine or not, human or not, input is always greater than the output. Atleast in case of humans the processing is spicier, we do not waste the energy on heat and sound like a robot, instead we spend it on our trifles or one can say even the real 'heat' "; he winks at me as he air quotes; "If you know what I mean"; he bites his lips like a naughty little teen boy. He is so stupid. I scoff before I start to dissent with him.
"What does that even mean?" Will narrows his eyes, he has no clue that Orleans just made a sexual innuendo. I do not blame him. You have to spend time with this dumbass before you can understand what is he even speaking.

"Bullshit! Sex is the single most contradiction to this theory. It leads to reproduction; and that shit ain't easy. In sex we put in the least effort while the output is a gigantic consuming machine. The output is almost like a living breathing company that is selfish, greedy and asks for more and more till it tires the parent out until one day it is feeding on its parent's leftovers and claiming it as its own. I completely disagree on that one. Nope – no no no. Now you see here the thermodynamics law doesn't work";
"You are wrong." Orleans says it with deep conviction.
"How?" I am curious as I see a smile slipping in on his face.
"You forgot the parent was the pre-output of the output itself before it became the parent. So that way the input by the parents of the pre-output was exhausting enough for the pre-output to perform the single most important job it was made ready to do. That is the right kind of sex that is done at the right time for copulation and tada! The pre-output is no more an output instead it becomes the input for the next output. And this output is once again in a loop served until one day it is ready to give a post-output"; he smirks.
I laugh. After all he might just not be that stupid.
"But I think this conversation is becoming one"; Shit! I look away immediately. How do I always forget that he could read me if I think and look into his eyes at the same time. How! HOW! HOW!
"Oh please, feel free to chose a sane conversation then"; this probably is going to be a bad idea.

I move closer to the door, trying to hear if mother was still in proximity. "I'd love to but I think your mother has an axe in her hands and we gotta get outta here before she chops us down and store us here in this dungeon-slash-janitor locker for no one to find us"; his nerves are hypervenlating.

"Gee! It's just an axe dude! Chill!" I try to listen harder. I can a blurry sound seeping through the thick door. Fuck she's playing *I will survive,* it means it's apology time!

Urgh! I groan.

 If I can hear the songs blazing in here, I guess she's back in her butcher room. The centre of this dungeon. When we were little and were grounded here, she used to play music and make me confess and apologise for my mistakes. I used to do it in the background of this particular song. She believes this song helps me collect power to confess my mistakes and strengthen me to have had survived my punishment down here in the dungeons. No wonder I ended up into this crazy bitch. Like mother like daughter! I remember each and every apology, I called it my Apology Room. The memories still send shudders down my spine. Tbh – now that I see, it really did help me grow as a strong woman. Look at me, no more afraid of dark dungeon lanes. No more afraid of actually confronting mother. I suppose it's time to embrace disobedience while my mother still conscious and agitated.

All this while I was begging to feel that am worth my mother's expectations, now I don't give a fuck. I had the woman tied and my father fooled. Now I don't want their validation. Now I want them to beg of mine.

I turn around; "Listen you two buttholes. Once we are outta here run. Take three left turns and two rights. Do it for five times, you will reach the end and will find stairs at the end of that dungeon lane. Climb and you'll reach mother's closet. Break her safe and there you will find your love potions. After that wait for me to get mom there. Complete your end of the deal and whoosh! – get out of my life for once and for all. You too Will"; Orleans look at me with incredulous eyes. Will on the other hand is busy chanting away; " three left – two right – five times – three left – two right – five times…"

"Why are you telling us that and not just lead us till there?" Orleans shut his mouth.

I sigh.

"Don't think that am all generous and putting my life at stake and shit. I am just doing this for myself. It's time my mother begs for my validation and not vice versa. So shut you smiling ass mouth up and run"; I slowly open the door. The song enters the room.

"Is that *I will survive* blazing through the dungeon walls?" Orleans asks with a furrow on his forehead.

I nod and tilt my head slightly; "That too on repeat"; I give him a lopsided smile.

"Fuck – your mom ruined the song for me"; Orleans make a disgusted face.

"She had it ruined it for me since the first time it ever was played"; I pout.

Orleans's stare lingers for more than twenty seconds, which kinda makes me awkward.

"I hope you make her fucking beg and whine on her knees, Salem"; he gives me a nod which I return him as a promise.

"Now get your ass outta here"; and there they run out the door.

I do a raspberry as I realise how inevitable my confrontation had become in this moment. If even I wish to back out, I'd risk Orleans's and Will's life. To get out of this hotch-potch, only one way is left. I gotta buy time enough for Orleans to reach the surface and make mother chase me to her closet and there complete what we started.

What I started.

Episode 39 - Salem

Genius has a way of being noticed. I always wanted to be a prodigy. I always wanted to be that genius. I always wanted to know the most, be the best – all that, without ever consciously doing any of that. I wished someone to genuinely believe in my genius, someone to actually understand me. Somebody to notice me. At the age of thirteen, I thankfully realised that I am among the desperates. Among those people who are fated to be alone – fuck fate, who am I kiddin' – I am among those people who would anytime prefer being alone and plotting to friendly and compliant.

I step back, take a deep breath in. The door is right in front of me; on the other side lies my master. The master whom I hate, but I am also thankful of, the master who taught and trained me to become what I am today.

Orleans and Will are long gone; all I've got to do is buy them next ten minutes so they can get out of this awful dungeon.

How did I end up being among these people? How?

Episode 40 – Salem

My dear old house. My dear dear old property. First it belonged to my grand-grand father, then to my grand father, then to grandmother, then to father and soon it will belong to me – officially and on paper. My grand house all dedicated to me. And I will make it sure that it comes all to me while and young and free, before my wrinkles show up and I need to get a botox and most importantly before I get married (if I get married). Apparently it's a big deal in this house. When we marry into someone's family, we aim to gain more than half of the power their corporation holds. And we never marry into families with no corporation. That would be sad, careless and quite frankly just tragic. Just imagine had anyone of my ancestors married stupidly or caused even the slightest of misjudgement regarding marital issues,they'd had end up ruining my golden future. Hell to rectify their judgement I'd had to make my engineers built a time machine, so I could personally go back and help them with the right decision. Or wait! Has the future-me already done that?
Well, it's most definitely possible. I mean, I can't stand stupidity and I abhor idiotic behaviours especially the ones that end up in ruination of my plans and my future (wait! Lemme make it clear) #MyFuture.
Period.

But I guess, my father doesn't care about me. He believes that he can outwit me and end me locked up in the lock of marriage while he'd enjoy magnificently in my glory days. Sadly, my father never talked to me. He never understood me like my mother does. He has the slightest clue that I am after all my grand father's blood and my mother's daughter. I am after all his death.

It was a week or two ago when I was walking down the house staff chambers. Everyone there is filthy petite. All look like those heroine-chick models who walk runways with their spines reaching out for air. Mother likes them that way. According to her, "it's worthless to be pomp and richness if not show pomp and richness. After all the taste of money is in all glamour and all play".

Yea! I know, she has weird concepts. But believe me, you'd gotta agree with her. What would you do just collecting money if you wouldn't want to spend it on the things you love? (and please all the activists and socialist, stop giving me answers! They are pathetic and desperate. Let's face it, we are all Satan's little bitches. If we get more, we want more, and then we want it more and more. It's called consumerism for crying out loud. The best kind of religion.

So, there I was walking down the chambers of my mother's house staff when suddenly my ears caught abhorrent words like; "marriage"; "coming of age"; "a woman"; and sadly; "Salem". That rung an alarming bell in my head. In fact it was the first time when I realised that I am a ticking bomb. And probably the worst kind of bomb – a kind of bomb that when explodes destroys itself and doesn't harm the immediate environment even an inch. I mean why would you even call that stupid thing a bomb! – but yea! It's a bomb. It's a bomb of that quantum level of feelings when a woman realises that her time has started, that if she wastes it or carelessly play with it like a foolish man; she'd end up exploding. And with that explosion will burst her career, her future and she herself. She'll either end up being married and family-frustrated or unmarried and society-frustrated. Frustrated, she will be. All she had to chose is which kind of flavour of frustration.

What a tragic story that sounds, right?

For years and years that has been the reality. We all know it, we've all seen it in our families. But no! Am not buying this shit. Am not a normal girl. Am not ending up being married to someone in order to help grow my father's empire, not unless the empire's horse reins lies in my hand. Nope. Not gonna happen. I have my own holy scripture, fun fact it has only one sentence in it:

"Fuck off from my way to conquering the world, Slothface!"

And this pretty much applies to both people and society.

Vixxi – 16

Oh please! There is nothing to be sad about the times you've been embarrassed. Don't listen to them, they don't know how to enjoy life, what they best know is meeting the norm. Now that is something they better get sad about.
Remember; it's better to be among those who if loves something will fall in deeply down for it.

Episode 41: Salem

There are more than a million ways I have had imagined confronting my mother after opening the door. I imagined her raining at me sharp knives, I imagined her thrashing me with her slippers, I imagined her choking me to death – worst case scenario – I imagined her actually listening to what I have to say. But what I see – what I see is far worse than my imagination.
"Tell me –"; Mother pauses. She is standing behind the butcher slab and chopping of the hog limb by limb. "Tell me little child what do you demand for dinner?" She is wearing her occasional apron. The apron she wears to cook special dinners.
I stay silent. *What the fuck is happening?* That is the first thought that pops up in my brain.
"Wha-wha-what do you mean?" I stutter as I slowly take a step forward but I never leave the doorway.

"Well, you better tell me what do you want to eat because dinner is soon to be and I need to cook it. Call your father, ask him what does he wishes to eat. I have to prepare that too"; she sighs and wipes her forehead with the back of her hand.

"Oh dear, I have so much to cook and so less time to have it all done"; *Chop!* There went the last limb. She took out the inner organs and remnants of the pig and threw them into the dustbin near the slab. Once thrown the unwanted parts she went back to butchering the whole thing.

"Mom"; a murmur like plea came out from my mouth. All the anger it subsided, for no reason a sense of pity started rising inside me. I can't have sympathy for this woman – this horrible austere woman who wishes nothing more than to ruin and dictate me.

"Stop"; another murmur escapes my lips. I am scared for her. Immensely scared.

"Oh Lovely I can't"; a chuckle follows her words. "I must get this complete before your father comes and discovers an empty dining table"; she is so focused on her work that it generates the feeling of sorry in me for her.

"Mom – please stop"; after a lot of gulping and assemblage of courage I finally speak out loud and clear.

She stops and slowly lifts her head to look at me; "Don't disturb me Salem. I need to get this work done with. Your father isn't a man of patience and I definitely am not a woman of tolerance. So.... shoo away I need to settle things down here in the kitchen"; and without another word she drops her head and continues her chopping.

Oh! This is bad. This is so bad! Inhale. Exhale!
I gulp and take another foot forward hesitantly moving away from the one and only escape door.
"Mother leave it to the chef, he will cook something nice for us all. Come out of here"; I speak.
Mother again looks up from her dead pig; "What part –"; she is losing her temper – I can tell – "What part of do not disturb me do you not understand?" she speaks with her jaw clenched.
I close my eyes; *Shit!* Exhale and open them back; she is waiting for my response. I can see the irritation in her eyes.
I hate this. I hate this. Now that she has generated pity for herself in me, once again my own issues are sidelined. As if all that matters are her reactions, her actions. When she'll wish she'll whip me; when she'll wish she'll sob; when she'll wish she'll hug me and when she'll wish she'll damn kill me. It's all about her – her – her. Be this, be that – so you can look like 'my' daughter. Read this – read that – so you can be 'my' daughter. Oh! You scored less on this exam – what did 'I' do to deserve such a daughter. Blah! Blah! Blah! All my fault and she's a fucking saint sacrificing her life for me. Well, you know what FUCK HER!
I breath heavily, I can hear myself gulping my saliva; "All bad girls stand up for themselves. All bad girls stand up for who they are. All bad girls are rejects and – rebels. All bad girls listen to themselves before they listen to others. All bad girls *fight*"; a strange kind of power overtakes me. Such hate – such hate – I could just never detach myself from such hate.
Mother looks up, away from her butchering and narrows her eyes.

"And if – "; my whole body pains – not physically but something like: it feels like a thousand metal rods beating me – beating my bones – beating me and my bones until they crack and crush.

"And if –"; I always wanted to be that good girl. To be that sweet sweet intelligent good girl. But I know what I am to this society more than I know who I am to myself. And this just fuels up my already flaring rage.

"And if that's what a bad girl is – then am proud to be one"; there I've said it out in the world, wasted my precious little words to these damped dungeon walls and to my mother's ever-deafened ears.

Mother stands still with the knife in her hand for quite a moment.

"Heh!" she snickers, was that bemusing to her? I think to myself. And a crescendo of snickery-laughter follows.

"You are as dumb as are the wits of a rabbit"; her laughter continues.

"Excuse me?" I stand very confused. In the background, suddenly the whole butchering table disappears and my mother's clothes change. Her apron and dress are turning into a shimmery gown – as if it is magic at work. *Is Orleans doing this?* I am too astounded to speak another word.

What is happening? Why is the room changing from a slaughter house into a decent place?

Mother finally notices my perplexed state of mind, which I am thoroughly accepting is reflecting in my expressions.

"I call it the Mad Dungeon"; she says as her fingers involuntarily reaches for the diamond locket that is suddenly adorning her neck.

"Mad Dungeon? Okay? What?" I take pause; "Umm – I don't get it"; I think my sanity is slipping away, which obviously looking at my mother right now explains why – it's the genes to blame! No offence meant there.

"I call it the Mad Dungeon. It helps me calm down. Makes me see things clearly. You know you can see the true nature of your emotions when they come alive. You see, that way you know what will help you build better and what will not"; she looks around.

I try looking at the scene around and to be completely honest I don't see it the way she sees it; "looks to me a nice place to dwell on your emotions as if they are as much alive to you as a friend would be to a person"; I comment. A rush of pity pause me from making fun of her anymore.

Mother looks at me with a clenched jaw.

She gulps. "You don't know what I've done for you and what I'll do for you"; she stiffly speaks.

"Don't you think that's the problem?" there, I say it out and loud. I am finally confroting my worst fears – talking about *my* emotions.

"Don't you think that you never letting your emotions out has belittled mine? Don't you think your acts of making me put guards ton my emotions like you clearly have done to yours has fucked me up?" I open my arms making her look at the Mad Dungeon walls around. The room suddenly turns dark. It is coming back to its state. The rosy-mossy smell dominating over the jasmine elite.

"I ask you of grandpa – why was I disciplined into standing on erect stools and fearing my grandpa? Why was I asked to never tell anybody what he used to do to me? Why you've blamed me for all that he did? Why all these years you've hated my guts? WHY HAVE YOU HATED ME WHEN YOU SHOULD HAVE HATED GRANDPA?" I couldn't anymore wait any longer to shout at mother and tear her apart with my questions.

"What are you talking about? I know nothing of the sort"; she eye rolls and turns away from me, the room darkens further.

"You knew mother – but you said that I deserved it. That it was my fault. That I was being punished. Why? Why? Why?"

"What are you speaking?" she was taking deep breaths.

"You deserved those whiplashes – your grandpa said you started liking them in the end. You are crazy"; she continues.

"I didn't like it – I never wanted to like it except my body reacted to it. That it becomes its habit. Grandpa's lash was on me and soon I felt as if I deserved its sting more than anything. Why did you let it happen and then pretend that it was my fault?"

I pause waiting for her to react.

When nothing leaves her lips, I crack open; "I am begging and begging and begging for you to finally come clean to me and answer me why my grandpa sexually assaulted me when I didn't even know of it – when I fucking thought it was all play until slowly my body started hating it";

I start to breath heavily; my heart starts to pound: it feels like a chained gate is being banged open inside me: It feels like all my hormones are crying into my blood.

"I wanted to stop my breath – puke all the time – wanted – and still wanna just kill myself but you know – you remember clearly what happened. My mind hated to disobey grandfather but my body hated to accept – I DON'T EVEN FUCKING REMEMBER WHAT HE USED TO DO EXCEPT FOR THE FUCKING FACT I USED TO FEEL LIKE SHIT AND SERIOUSLY DEAD!"

"SHUT UP! SHUT UP! I WAS SAVING YOUR FATHER!" Suddenly lightening claps in front of me inside the dungeon and the thundering sound follows, in fright I step back a bit. My mother finally opens her mouth;

"Children don't understand their feelings. Their memories aren't reliable. But you had to remember for some damn-cursed reason. You had to remember when I thought I'd protect you from those memories by honing you into a lady – by – by eliminating your grandfather – But NO – nononono – You *had* to remember what your grandfather did to you –";

She pauses, her eyes goes back to the knife; her fingers tracing the sharp edge of the butchering tool.

"He did the same to your father – your father , he used to come to the oak tree and he used to cry. He couldn't understand what used to happen to him. One day I saw Mr. Enoch in his terrible fit; I saw what he did to your father. It was excruciating – completely horrible. I didn't know what to do. I couldn't stop it from happening but – but I was there next to your father all along – all the time. I was too scared and too – too frightened to tell my own mother. Back home my father used to place the same wrath on my mother. "But one day my father stopped assaulting my mother in all manners and I learnt – I learnt it was a witch's doing" she takes in stuttering breaths before she continues; "I was too stupid – at that moment it was better for me to be stupid than scared. So – I went to the witch"; she licks her lips; "and made a deal". "Deal?" my eyebrows raises. That struck me like lightening out of the blue.
"Yes – a deal – that your grandfather won't touch your father if I gave them my first born son"; she again takes a deep breath; "and that is the reason why it became imperative for your father to have married me"; her chest rises and falls in shaky-crescendos; "I swear, I never planned to trap your father into this nuptial – I just wanted to save him. His money was nothing to me – but I was poor, and no matter how innocent a human would come to be, hope for a better future is always found tempting. Do not blame me like your father does. I saved him life for god's sake. But nah! Instead of being thankful and genuine he comes out to be blaming and taunting"; her eyes fill with salty tears – wow, she's crying, like genuinely crying – wow!

"Anyway – I made the deal and your father married me. Your grandfather's fits lessened and your father was quiet grateful for that year. But soon I got pregnant – pregnant with a daughter – I aborted"; she looks at me... regretfully? Blamingly? Hatefully? Hard to decipher from her constant angry glares.
"I could have stayed happy with a girl in another life. In a life where the fates hadn't already coded the system against a daughter. I impregnated myself again – I found it was a girl. I aborted – 8 month abortion. Now that was dangerous at that time.
"I impregnated again – again a girl – a girl a girl a girl – it felt like a *curse!*" mother shouts in my face.
"The witches were left unhappy and unsatisfied. Your grandfather started again with his violent fits. But sadly this time, your father didn't cry – sadly he learnt the husband's trick"; mother's eye went blood-shot red.
"Men's trick?" I repeat
"Yea! – when a man becomes husband, he doesn't suffer alone – he *shares* – he shares his pain"; mother presses her lips tightly and in the most pitiful manner she looks at me with a pair of sad eyes and a daunting smile.
"I started becoming the victim. Now, that was not in any of the deals made – by deal or by vow – thrashing and subduing and extremist bullying was never written in any of those. But there it was – a side-effect – oh no – a by-product of all those deals and vows and goddamn *sharing!*" she closes her fingers into a fist and beats it on the table.

"Those were the worst days of my lives; worse than poverty; worse than a death sentence. You love that person but you know that that person will kill you, you want to save that person but you wanna thrash his head and make him feel like he's making feel you – can you comprehend that feeling? Huh? Huh? Can you?"
She looks at me, her eyes wild with the terror of those flashbacks. My eyes suddenly swell; *I comprehend – I comprehend well mother*, I wish to speak but all I can do is part my lips in search for breath.
"So I went to the witches again. I struck another deal. A deal that consisted of love potions and your grandfather's fits they said. I didn't understand them at all. But now I get it"; she pauses;
 "I guess"; her eyes wander around, away from me they stay on the walls. Her fingers lift up and I know she's wiping her tears away.
"I don't understand"; I speak my thought.
"I went there to ask for an alternative way. Anything but another abortion. To that they gave me a love potion and they whispered to me '*the child will bear it all*'I did as I was told. And then came you. A girl, but a girl with a purpose. You have been such a rebel, such a leaf against the wind that it drove me crazy. You were supposed to bear all our sorrows but you just grew and grew into such nasty tantrums that it became impossible for me to make peace in this family. And then I decided." She took an assertive pause. Not a single person would believe looking at her at that moment that she'd been crying a minute ago.

"You couldn't keep your mouth shut about how horrible your grandfather was – you just couldn't. Everyone was afraid of you back talk and I was blamed for *aalll* of it. I – the one who wished to save you and your father – who wished to save this family. So I had to do what I had to do. When witches don't come to use, humans better embrace their utilitarian duty. To avoid the worst the best had to be eliminated or it would become a cannibal in no time. Your grandfather died. The family mourned, but afterwards the family grew. Your father changed for the better. *I* changed for the better"; she pauses.

"So tell me, tell me – I saved you. I bloody well saved you from that monster"; *FML but this is now going way over my patience level – Stop it mother – stop it;* "But NO! You don't know how to control your anxiety let alone your memories"; *STOPP – STOUUUHHHPPP – STOP stop stop stop stop;* "Why can't you understand!" *Stop – oh fuck this is killing me;* "Filter of forgetting is essential for one to move on in life. For one to have a better future";

I take in a deep breath.

"Mother"; I almost whisper-growl. Numb – numb – numb – numb – that's what I feel – numb – I feel no sadness for mother, nothing for nobody – just numb – fuck they can't feel for me, I can't feel foe them. That's the first law of bargain.

Right now, all I wanna do is go back and eat that pizza – take that pistol out of my father's locker and shoot myself until am as numb as I am right now. But – tahtahtahtah! – nope – can't miss the prom – it's important for my insta feed, plus I don't want to give anybody even a speck of chance of making me a tragedy. Because am not. I refuse to be one. I'll be a legend – I'll be a cursed villain – worst case scenario somebody's inspiration but NOT – A – TRAGEDY. "Mother – father is cheating on you"; Yea! That's how I release a highly compressed anger – in my numb way; "That too with me"; her jaw drops, I quickly need to clarify; "But he doesn't know that"; now she's just constipated confused.

"Also, please just abandon me – go somewhere far far away from me before I go full-throttle on you. 'Cause I know in the following moments I would love to make you feel exactly the way you are making me feel right now. I wish this Mad Dungeon does that to you. I wish it plays with your head so hard – so hard that you finally forget how horrible you are as an example of a saviour. At least that way you'll stop glorifying your acts and yourself"; I wish to spit on her face. Suddenly a tile in the roof moves and a dark mouth opens above mother's head. A water like substance comes vomiting down the cell.

"What is this sticky-thing?" Mother shouts, horrified at what just happened.

I stifle my smile. Didn't expect the Mad Dungeon would respond to my wish.

She looks at me after realising what had just happened.

"Oh no – don't – don't think anything worse of me – believe me this place will gnaw at you and your feelings like the sad pages of someone's diary"; she warns me but I can't help but wish to chop her tongue off, but I don't actually want to – but...

Suddenly knives come out of nowhere and start to circle around mother's neck and starting revolving around it. First they revolve slowly; it feels so satisfactory to just look at her scared face. I can draw such immense satisfaction looking at those knives tease her – never touching her skin but coarsely caressing her of impending pain – but never, never letting her feel it. The knives drop.

She exhales sharply, her neck red with the tease. Her eyes blood-shot, she glares at me; "What was that?" I smirk, cock my head and with the most taunting smile say; "I just saved you mother, be *grateful*" there – wow – that is called cathartic experience – let her have the taste of her own words.

Unfortunately, only for a while could I savour this moment.

Ding! Dong!

That takes both of our attention.

"Who's that?" I ask to myself.

"That's your father"; mother replies, my head turns to her; she's looking at her phone and electronically opening the door.

"Shit! Orleans!" I turn around, ready for a run.

"Oh! That poor boy – he's dead. And the sad part is nobody will care"; My – my! the audacity this woman has!

"You will never be able to reach in time"; she says and the door immediately starts to brick. I skid as I stop myself from banging into the wall. She confines us in the Mad Dungeon.

"Mother – I need to go – I must"; I plead her as I face her.

" He – he can't die. Please, I got him into all this – I am the one at fault here. Unlike you"; I try to keep sarcasm out of my voice; "I accept that I did wrong. Please do not punish him for my mistakes. Pleaaassee open the wall"; After a long – long time she feel warm tears meet her cheek; "But I also do accept what I don't understand is your pathetic ungratefulness"; I look at the wall and murmur; "Can't be reasonable at all"; I give up – I can't mother out. I am exhausted. I feel like my anger is grabbing me and making me mad and like a wrecking ball its hitting the damn wall wide open. Never – never have I felt so mad.

Some rooms, despite their inanimate bricks and walls and tiles are too cursed to stay dead. They are alive because we want them to be alive, because we want them to be as alive as our brains are. Because we want to see what our minds look like in physical-reality.

"I get it now – I get grandma's story; she died of old age, but she said she died of obesity, maybe both, I don't know. But I get it now. You see, for some it's a tragedy; for my grandmother it's how you sell a story. I get it from where do you get your tendency to stay justify all your acts. And am sorry that you had to go through all that fuckery. But – but don't mistake it for even a second that I will let you justify all this. 'Cause I swear – I swear I'm mad enough to chop your cores piece by piece"; my jaw clenches; "*atom by atom*". The wall cracks and in no second I run for Orleans.

Vixxi - 17

It is interesting how most of us fail to understand the beauty of oneself. We let our repressed emotions burst out at an unusual time or place rather actually deal with them in the moment we realise their presence. Life is an opportunity to realise ourselves; not a divine gift to spend on fitting in the society, or believing in a cause that people around believe in. Life is a challenge and it is extremely difficult to embrace life as an independent opportunity. But imagine, imagine what if it is? After all we are all movies and we all star in them and sometimes also do crossovers in others' too.

Episode 42: Orleans

My panting can't stop. Will is even more out of breath. Poor soul! Never in a million years had he thought that he would get burnt and threatened to death on the very same day and that too in an ancient dungeon.
"Salem's still back there"; after all we went through; he's still worried about Salem? Bitch! She deserves to rot in that dungeon as much as that mother of hers. But – well – she *is* trying to save us, so maybe not as much as her mother.
And of course I won't let that happen! She's my friend now. That changes everything; "She'll be okay! She needs to confront her dear mother and sort out some issues of her before she surfaces back again"; I simply reply with my casual tone.
My feet involuntarily get back up on the ground. I look around; another immaculate white room. Who knows what treasures are hidden here.

"What is this place?" Will asks as he follows behind.
"Exactly my thought"; there are just walls around here – white, fancy walls. A pentagon shaped room with a single rectangular white leather made mini couch cum seat, placed in the center of the room.
"Wow!" Will exclaimed.
"I know"; I agree in complete hypnotism.
"How badly did I burn?" Will asks. Why is he asking me that right now?
I look at him with a creased forehead, and make a sibilant sound.
"Forget it, don't answer that"; he lets me go. He isn't looking at the white walls anymore. His eyes are sparkling with reflected light. I turn to see the wall behind me. There stands the largest looking glass in front of me. Apparently it's also a secret door to the dungeons.
"Everything's white and reflective. I swear this place has some really stupid rooms"; Will snickers as his eyes wander abou –
Wait!
It's not a stupid room! Of course it's white and reflective! Because it's the master closet. I turn around. I swear one could see a hopeful glitter in the corner of my eyes and a bursting aura radiating from my body.
"My love potions! Never my words have hold so much hope as these three did. I run to one of the four white walls. There must be a knob somewhere.
"What are you searching?" Will asks with amusement. Obviously cherishing my uncanny behaviour.
"It's a closet"; I tell him awkwardly.
"Okay! Sooo..." he elongates the 'o' in 'so'.

"So? So I need to find a way to open this thing and find my thing and whoosh! Get away from this family and its crazy members as far as possible"; I exhale a deep breath.

"Now for that – I'll find a whole new universe for you if you need it"; Will casually chuckles but I – I pause. Nobody has ever said that to me (and yes we are NOT including mom). His words – it felt as if his words – his words just quaked my whole world.

"What? – now don't literally ask me to get a universe for you"; he chuckles.

I shake my head. Something rushed in me. A tinge of fear mixed with a lot of excitement exploding inside my chest with a lot of joy.

Wow!

That's a beautiful feeling!

"Nothing"; I quickly look away from him. Mostly to hide my evident blush but also to remind myself the impossibility of the feeling that is blooming within me. Marco's presence makes me feel the same but it soon fades away. Like a sweet smell faded in air. But the manifestation of this feeling is like a manifestation of a sweet memory in the smell of that air.

I try focusing on his actions rather thinking about him like a record player on a roll. He presses the wall. A blue light lights on the margins, edges and two in the middle. The wall breaks into two rectangular halves and slide as their ends on the hinge sides folds like folds of a blind.

The beautiful wall open into the biggest walk-in wardrobe I've ever behold.

Will moves around and just like he opened this wardrobe; he opens the other three walls. Apparently the fourth wall leads outside the closet and into the master bedroom.

"WOAH! It's like Paris in here!"; I clap my hands together and spin around in excitement.

I take out a yellow fur and a big diamond choker. My hands can't control but slip them over my skin. The beautiful young fur and the old ancient diamond magnificently worn. This. This is what beauty is like. Rich and beyond my budget. The thought simply brings a frown on me.

I look over to Will; he's just perfectly calm around all this. He sits on the leather mini couch in the center. He checks out the different kind of buttons embedded in the control panel fixated on the inner side of the couch's arm. He clicks something here and there – and *viola!* Out comes a slightly cold slide containing ostentatious vintage champagne bottles with champagne glasses on the side.

A smile flourishes over Will. I raise my eyebrow – this is impressive. I crouch down and move my fingers over the cold glass of the bottles like mallets hitting the metal bars of a xylophone. My blood starts dancing with the touch of a new bottle; "What a waste..." I murmur; "Not a single one opened";

"I don't know shit about chateau – but all this looks something like am never gonna have one"; he takes out one bottle and gently rolls it around to admire it closely. My eyes are all set on the champagne bottle he is playing with.

He rips off the seal with his still good hand and smirks; "Wanna get bubbly?"

I can feel my lips turn into a Cheshire smile as I quote my style icon; "Abso-fucking-lutely"; I bite my lower lips and wiggle my eyebrows as I share my thoughts. While he opens the bottle, I take out glasses; he pours the champagne. The bubbles excite me as they pop. I look at Will and he's about to take his first sip; "Oh no – no"; I stop him before he commits the horrible act of sipping without a toast.
"What?" he asks, a bit bewildered of me stopping him from taking his sip.
"You can't do it without a toast"; I give him the most condescending look possible; as if he should be ashamed or rather die before having had done what he was about to.
"Why?" he raises his eyebrow and shrugs his shoulder.
"Why? – "; I am taken aback, and that I make very evident with my expressions; "Please Will! Do as the clique do"; I roll my eyes, exhale in disappointment; and here I thought I could find in him a potential lover.
"To…"; I take time to think as I raise my glass
"To forgetting this night as soon as possible"; Will completes for me, and that too very neatly.
I smile; "Can't be suffice enough"; we clink our glasses and take a deeply delicate-enlighteningly conscious sip. My eyes close as I try living the moment.
"Why do people make toasts?" Will asks.
I open my eyes, stand up and move to the mirror. I feel glamorous, empowered, beautiful and strong; "I don't know it's the way of the world I guess"; I take another sip; my eyes wander to the footwear; a pair of green Vuitton hits my eyes.
I want them!

A strange desire hits me. I take them out and as I wear them I answer him; "there's this one account where it says that people in ancient times toasted to check if there was no poison in their drink. You see, when the glasses clinked, the drinks spilled into each other, thereby asserting you are dead if you spiked my drink"; once am done, I stand and walk to the mirror – AH! AM DELIGHTED.

Will is laughing at the stupid culture we humans have inherited.

I give him a side glance and critique; "you can't call them stupid when you live off a teen girl's pizza fantasy"; he scoffs politely; "Whatever dude! It still is stupid";he gets up and starts walking around the room. I ignore him and bring my attention to the mirror again.

"What's this?" Will asks from the other end of the room, I look from the mirror. He has opened Mr. Enoch's wardrobe and there is this record player set in the middle. He crouches down and takes out a vintage album cover from a whole shelf of vinyl records; "I know only this girl"; he takes the album out and inserts in the record player.

"And to be frank, I know only one song on this thing"; I take another sip as Will talks out loud. My legs take me to the vanity; I sit on the stool and look at myself in the mirror. My eyes are reflecting diamond. I inspect the desk; everything seems so expensive – everything seems so Dior and Chanel.

"Oh! Her today's cologne is here"; I say raining the bottle. Will is pretty busy with the record player, so he ignores me. I take a look at the small sparkly bottle; "Oh! If only we had thought to check the vanity!" I sigh.

I open the bottle and spray it over me.

Ah! Yes that smells expensive. I bite my lips.

I place the bottle on the desk. My fingers roll onto a lipstick. I uncap it and unroll it. It's red and dark. I handle it with care as I paint my lips red.

"Finally! Got it"; Will exclaims in achievement, as Summer Wine by Nancy Sinatra starts playing in the background.

I don't know – it's an ecstatic feeling.

My diamond neck, my yellow fur, my green heels, my drunken eyes, my red lips and among them – my tattered old men's jeans. I chuckle looking at it.

I get up and again look at myself in the long mirror.

"Wow! You look –"; He takes a mini break as his eyes check me out head to toes; "Amazing"; he takes another sip. A sudden shudder of happiness surges through my blood.

It's purely electric – this – this – this feeling, it's amazing – wonderful – beautiful and so exploding. I chuckle; everything just adds to this moment – this beautiful moment, where am not afraid of being me. This moment where I don't care. I don't care. I – DON'T – FUCKING – CARE!

I spin around again in absolute glee. I look so beautiful.

"Whoa! Whoa! Whoa! Slow down there Mr. Broadway Show!" Will again gives away his series of chuckles. I wish I could box them. I press my lips tight, stifling a chuckle of my own. I wish I could box this whole moment.

"You're so high on snorting diamonds on fur"; he teases me.

"Stop being so jealous. I know I look fabulous"; to mask my shyness I raise my chin and fan my hand under it.

It feels like a century has passed as we sit here laughing, talking, teasing, adorning expensive clothes and making a memory.

Never had I thought how much on a sensitive precipice this moment would stand. How much to a terrifying but revolutionising moment it would lead. Because this single memory is followed or rather is shattered by a single lash of a leather belt that neither of us saw coming.

It has been over an hour. Salem has still not arrived. Will is almost done with the whole bottle of champagne. I look over to the door leading to the dungeon.

Where is she? What is taking her this long?

I step closer to the mouth of the stairs when *wuh-psssh!* I hear the whip crack.

My head turns around as Will screams. He is crawling on the ground, his drink stains the couch; he crawls away from man with the whip.

Mr. Enoch has caught us playing and he doesn't like it.

Vixxi – 18

Today she is on that side of the table. Today he is judging her. Today he is sitting on a higher seat and today she is seated on the lower ground. Today she has to look up to meet his eyes. Today it is all his and alls her to do. But don't forget today is ending by each minute passing by and tomorrow will come. Tomorrow she will be seated there and tomorrow she will be on a higher seat, a seat made by her for her, a seat that will become a part of her. Tomorrow is just a midnight away. Be as happy as you can be today, you only have minutes left. Because tomorrow is the end and tomorrow will become the present and then it will be her turn – her turn to sentence you, forgive you; her turn to listen to you or throw you down; her turn to point a finger at you or protect you. Tomorrow it will be her turn and you – darling you will suffer the consequences of the judgments made by you today.

Episode 43: Salem

I run as fast as I can, mother is behind me. Neither she nor I are anymore thinking of killing each other. On both of our minds lies the fear of father finding Orleans and Will out – well that's what's on my brain; my mother's mind must be on him finding the house in distress.

I can see the stairs. I take long leaps to reach them. I hastily step on the stairs and take longer leaps to reach the mouth opening out these dingy dungeons. I can hear mother pant behind me. I can even hear shouts. Music is coming from the entrance. There is white light and – *Aaahhhhh!!*
My heart beats quicken, I stop, I look behind at my mother. She has also stopped, her face is bright red. I gulp before I run in fear. I can hear the whip crack. Shit! What have you done father.
As I take my first step to the door entrance I know before I see what is happening and what is going to happen.

Episode 44: Orleans

There are some moments in life – some moments in life that seem perfectly calculated but in fact are purely accidental in nature.
Something alike is the case when Mr. Enoch tried murdering me. It was like a siege of terror had gripped my heart; as if in that moment I would lose the most precious thing in my life – my life.
I never felt such experience brush past me, I never would want such experience to ever brush pass me. It's terrible but quite frankly it feels like a nightmare. A horrifying lucid dream but a dream from which you can wake up from. And that night I wished to wake up – wake up so bad.
Wuh-psssh!
Wuh-psssh!
Wuh-psssh!
Wuh-psssh!

I will remember this moment vividly – clear as crystal. This moment when terror marks you and drags you from zenith to nadir. This moment when am all curled up and shivering and crying and feeling pathetic and guilty for no reason at all. This moment when am feeling pathetic and so weak and so much at crime when all I've done is be me – that's all.
I will remember this sound;
Wuh-psssh!
This sound that impresses on me terror – that impresses on me fear – this sound that makes me open a dark room and cry in its dark corners – this sound that blurs light – this sound that strikes – this sound that makes me convulse in pain – this sound that sends through my veins a feeling so timid in nature that it makes me hate myself – this sound that is stripping me naked – this sound that fills me with utter shame – this sound that makes me feel guilty – this sound – this sound that has no meaning to most is sentencing me as hated, rejected – as... as... as unloved. Mr. Encoh bends down takes me by the furcoat's collar and looks at me with red angry eyes; "How dare you? HOW DARE YOU WORE CLOTHES THAT I BOUGHT FOR MY WIFE?" with grit teeth he looked at me with mad eyes. I shiver and tremble in panic, trying to get myself out of the fur. Mr. Enoch grabs me by the arm and tightens his grip. I cry out loud in pain. I cannot save myself, I just realise I cannot save myself. In that moment; fear has gripped my neck so tight that no rational thought surfaces. "Disgusting creatures! I will not tolerate this"; he squeezes my jaw with his fingers, I cannot stop but cry; "Stop – please STOP!"

"Oh I will"; he throws me down like garbage, gets up and goes to his wardrobe drawer. All the feelings seem to come in a rush. I cough, blood spills out of my upper lip. I touch my nose, blood is rushing out of my nostrils. I try to stand up, by my arms – my ribs; they feel exhausted, they are in pain.
I look above; Mr. Enoch is doing something inside the drawers.
Will is in the corner with his eyes wide. He is stunned. Petrified.
He doesn't know what hit us.
I look back at Mr. Enoch, coughing and whining in pain; again a surge of thousand feelings surface.
But this time I can feel – two feelings in specific: Shame and Hatred. Pure hatred.
He turns around, his right hand still inside the drawer but his eyes are glaring at me. I try crawling to the couch. There is a metal plate inside the champagne set. I'll bash his brains out if he hits me again.
"I can't tolerate people like you. It just means encouraging people to go against the norms of the nature. No – I cannot"; he takes his hands out of the drawer and in his hand is a revolver. I quicken my crawl to the metal plate.
"You will thank me one day for this"; he raises his revolver.

Nope – I was wrong before – this is fear – this is fear in its raw form. This is what death looks like; omnipresent while you are helpless and struggling to find a way out. I can see my heart start beat at godspeed as Mr. Enoch pulls his trigger. I can feel my breath quicken as I realise how low are my chances at surviving. My hands stretch out to take the plate out when Mr. Enoch pulls the trigger.

BANG!

In that second I know am done.

My eyes close automatically.

Thakhhhh!

My face crinkles at the sound anticipating the hit and pain. As far as I know, bullets hit first and then they make sound. But nothing. It's been more than a second since the sound came. Something's wrong.

I open my eyes; the metal plate is floating in front of me with a dent in its bottom side. My gaze shifts, the bullet is still racing towards Mr. Enoch. The realisation that my magic saved me – strike that – the realisation that my **curse** saved me strangely makes me feel like a living anomaly. How can I forget, I am a fucking immortal, and here I was dramatic and shit.

Kheecheeek!

A piercing sound comes and at the same time the plate drops, my eyes look at the source of the noise. *Ouch!* I exclaim inside my brain; the bullet pierced through Mr. Enoch's crotch and probably hit him in his balls. Poor thing! My teeth hiss at the idea. Mr. Enoch falls backward with the force.

BANG!

Another gunshot. This time, the bullet hits the roof almost just above Mr. Enoch's falling body. The roof cement cracks; I snap my finger; and a huge chunk of roof cement falls on the now-fallen-body of Mr. Enoch. The huge layer of white-grey cement crushes him.

That's for hitting me.

I snap my fingers again; another small chunk of roof cement drops and hits (where I believe lies Mr. Enoch's face) and bashes his brains out.

"That's for calling me disguting"; I whisper to myself. I release a sigh of breath and close my eyes. My ears are still buzzing with gunshots and screams. I didn't know when Salem and Ms. Enoch had come; but I think that they were here long enough to see him die. I hope they were here to see him die.

My body is still on the floor; in pain and in suffer. My head is spinning; I can't express but feel the million feelings exploding in my chest.

People are screaming around me in agony. I can feel Salem brush past me. Ms Enoch collapses behind me. Nothing stirs me.

I just want to get outta here.

"What did you do Axel? What did you doooo?" Salem shouts from the far end where his father's fresh corpse lies.

It takes me pains to open my tightly shut eyes; in anger when I do open them. I try sitting; it's painful; my eyes dart straight at Salem and the pile of rocks covering Mr. Enoch's body.

"I..." a strange gush of energy tries to escape each and every bone in me – it electrifies each and every vein in me – as if this energy would burst me into flames; "I – "; I grit my teeth.

"I –"; I raise my fingers toward him and speak with rage and fury; "I curse your father to an eternal sleep where he becomes what he finds disgusting".

"And what will that do, you moron?" Salem cries back. She isn't crying, she's just angry.

"Teach him to respect"; I blankly respond; my body is torpid. I feel nothing, all those feelings that were gushing through me a minute ago have stopped.

Episode 45: Salem

I conclude: If this were a song; it'd be a Nightcore on YouTube.

Those are the best kind of songs; so much – much – much better than any contemporary pop.

Just like this murder; raw, rough, pathetic and poetic.

Like a blank verse; this murder is plain.

And so it can easily be shown as an accident.

Vixxi – 19

Someone had an awful dream, an awful – awful dream. A dream where someone burnt and burnt and burnt someone's room, again and again. Each time someone'd give it a new style and each time someone would burn it to give it a better one. But someone never liked it and somehow someone's walls never burnt down to ash with the fire. They'd still stay of the same colour someone'd last painted, they'd still have the same tile but with just a hint of candle waste on the tile or shedding of the outer layer of concrete in patches. However, someone never found any trace from where did the candle came from. Intriguing right? Well at least to someone it was. The dream was so vivid that by the end of it someone'd completely forgotten that burning someone's room is not a normal act to proceed with. That burning someone's room has consequences – major fatal consequences. All someone cared about was burning it and redecorating it. Here pink – here blue. Here that tile here that marble – here that ply here that plaster. That's it – that's all someone dreamt.

Episode 46: Salem

DNA helixes.
We are all bound to reproduce more and more improved (well strike that) sluggier versions of DNA helixes. In simple words – reproduction.

Well thanks to that information, I do not feel mandatory to feel a single drop of guilt for starting this all. I look back at my father's crushed body. It is a piece of art if at all it is anything.

Oh fuck!

Something warm drips down my cheek; my fingers in a reflex touch it. *Invisible tears!* That's what I call them

Wow!

I can't believe that there are tears rolling down my cheeks. It's a Christmas miracle on a day of Hallo-week.

Until now.

A single tear rolls down my eye, as I see blood flooding out of my father's crushed skull that lies beneath this cement. I am careful to not wet my hands in his blood; that's just being stupid enough to leave evidence.

"AAAAAAAHHHHH..." someone shrieks behind me. Probably mother.

"I'm sorry"; I murmur to myself hoping my father will listen at least the sound of it.

My whole body is on my knees; my head is hovering over my father's cement-masked face. My world is pretty gory at the moment. Everything around me blurs; the shrieks, the voices, the commands, the shouts yadayadayada...

But I feel at contradiction; as if my mind is saying something else but my lips are acting different. There are so many paradoxical feelings clouding my actions at the moment that am afraid to say that – that – I *feel!* I feel as if am dying from inside. Not dead. Dying. I've never felt so.

I've always felt dead. Dying? That's not a feeling am familiar with and neither is it the feeling I wish to be familiar with.

But why am I feeling like dying? It's definetly not my father's death that is making me feel unsettled. It's definitely not his cold body that shivers me to the spine. Then what is it? I look away from my father's dead eyes and find Orleans trembling.

He's trying to get up, to get on his feet; his face is red – as if any moment now the blood will explode his face into pieces like a ticking bomb. I look into his eyes. Yes. That's what is making me feel like dying. Fear. But his fear is very different from my fear. He is suffering from the fear of almost dying and I – well am scared of the future. Scared of what will happen next. Scared that the man who owns the house lies dead in front of my eyes and this will lead to an investigation, an investigation that will lead to invasion of dad's private life, which will lead to Amanda. And Amanda will lead to me.

But am feeling relieved too! This is so confusing! Urgh! What is happening – why am I feeling as if a hot metal iron is poking my chest or as if a thousand small needles are pinned to my heart.

"Daa – ad?" I speak a bit with strength. All my words come in quakes. I don't understand. Why am I feeling this? It was important. His death – it was important and it was his own doing – but it happened at the wrong time in the wrong place.

I can hear my breath.

It's deep and... *shivery?*

Only one thought runs through my brain as my tears roll down in the act of remorse and shock; *how will I make this look like it wasn't a murder?*
I look back at a very petrified Orleans.
I scan the room; mother is on the floor; looking helpless and acting melancholic. Will is crouching against one of the closets; his head and hands over his knees; he's swinging back and forth in utter alarm.
I wipe my tears; get up; open mother's vanity closet; pick up mother's fine comb and start walking.
All three of them are in intense shock; none of them are paying attention on me. I walk over to Orleans; stop – for a whole minute I stare at him; but he doesn't acknowledge me at all. I can listen to his heart run a marathon.
I walk a bit more and stand over mother. Her head turns toward me, she is breaking mentally. Her eyes are begging me to reverse time; his lips are quaking in fear and desolation. She is oblivious to a life without her husband. Not that she isn't aware of how much more advantageous is this death going to prove for us; it's just that she just lost the last person alive who knew her heart and soul; through and through.
"He- he is ac-actually d-d-dead"; she stutters.
I nod.
"How did this happen?" she whispers as she looks back at her husband's corpse from two tiles away.
"It was an accident mother; he was trying to rape you, so you had pull the gun on him"; I spoke like a reporter informing town folks on a news channel.
My mother's head jerk to look at me. Will's head turned toward me, my words even had Orleans attention.

"What? What do you mean?" mother asks, she start to get up on her feet.

"I mean you had several skull injuries as father tried to rape you, but before he could you shot him in self-defence. But sadly you remember nothing. Reasons diagonised will be PTSD and skull injury"; I detail my plan out loud.

"What do you mean? What are you trying to sell here?" she stands up straight, looking at me in confusion.

I smile; "I am trying to sell a story that will save us all – including you"; her forehead crease turn into angry dents; but before she'd utter a single vicious word, I raise mother's comb and with full throttle bash her skull with its metal end.

"WHAT THE FUCK?" Will screams. He squeals away in a crawl away from me – or nearer to the escape door.

Orleans stays silent. Not a word leaves his lips.

He looks at my unconscious mom; collapsed once again on the floor and then his eyes meet mine.

Thank me later

I speak to him.

"Settle the deal"; I say out loud.

He licks his lips, does not care to stand up, he slides with his knees, comes closer to mother.

"You both are crazy"; Will shouts in the background.

He bends his head over her, chants some words, brings his lips over her forehead and kisses it. His lips stay there for more than a few second. Once he's done. He stands up, not a single expression leaves his face. He's blank as a pole in the dark.

"My potions"; he says with nothing more than a whisper.

I gulp; I leave my parent's closet. I always admired the master bedroom. Entering it makes me realise that my father will never sleep here ever again. It's creepy. I shake away the thought and focus on finding my mother's cell phone.

My dear dear stupid mother, how she unknowingly told me the password. I find my mother's phone on her bed table.

I enter back inside the closet. Orleans is waiting for me, I know he is even when he has become incapable of reacting. He'll get through this. I know he will.

I walk toward my mother, crouch over her body; place the phone to detect her face – and *click!* The phone unlocks.

I open her MagApp; scroll down to her notifications and there the newly generated five-minute valid password pops on the screen.

I know where mother last put her magic potions. I go to the wardrobe; open the doors. I step inside; slide the hanging clothes and find a sliding door. I slide it and there in the middle of the wall is fixated a metal locker; safeguarded by both metal and magic. I put in the pin and *bingo!* The drawer opens.

The love potion box rests inside the drawer.

I can feel Orleans eyes on me. I hesitate a moment before I dive inside the metal safe and bring the box out. The box is a beautiful antique piece.

I admire it for more than a moment. It's beautiful. It's so precious and beautiful. It has bottles that can make mother love me or – or – or even better, it can make me love someone.

Snap!

A click of fingers and just like that my dreams shatter. I turn around and Orleans is walking away with the box out the door.

"Wait! Where are you going?" I step outside the closet and follow him. Will runs after him too.

"Where are you two going?" I ask again.

"I've had more than what I came for – so am leaving"; Will clears it.

"A word to anyone and Orleans will magically mute you forever"; I give him my warning eye.

Orleans halts; "You don't have to say that, in fact am sure he's more afraid of you than he'd ever be of me"; he looks at me and then Will. At that moment I see genuine fear in Will's eyes for me.

"Whatever"; I roll my eyes in dejection.

"Anyway, where do you think you're going leaving me here all alone?" I don't like him leaving me here alone.

"I am going to my fucking bed – to my fucking Timothee Chalamet!" he shouts at me and takes an about turn.

This angers me.

I step closer to him and narrow; "For your kind information, you got no right yelling around and showing tantrums around me when YOU ARE THE ONE FUCKING KILLING MY FATHER!" I shout in his face – like literally *in* his face.

His eyes widen.

"Excuse me?" he is in acute surprise.

"Oh hell yes Orleans Axel. You fucking killed my father; you owe me a lifetime's debt"; I believe he is being finely charged with appropriate accusations.

"Are you blind? Didn't you see him pulling the trigger on me? I am the victim here"; he reddens again, his eyes are furious with anger.

"Are *you* blind? 'Cause as far as I know, you were the one with the metal plate – you intentionally positioned it in such a manner that it would mark him as a hit"; I look at him with a clenched jaw and unwavering eyes. In a reflex to my response; Orleans leaves his one hand from his love potion box and his fingers find combing his hair and harshly massaging his forehead.

"Salem –"; Will speaks. I look at him with a side-eyes. His eyebrows are stitched and he looks at me with a funny expression; "Has anyone ever told you that you have a potential of one day becoming a really good lawyer?" where did that come from? I raise my eyes, smirk to one-side.

"I think so too"; and wink at him.

"Think so too? That-that's what's coming out of your shitty mouth"; Orleans again starts shouting at me. I roll my eyes.

"Oh please! Stop with all that drama – and help me out here"; I look at him with drooping eyelids.

"Help you out? Fuck you Salem! Fuck you!" he turns around and again starts walking out.

Will follows him.

"My plan is easy Orleans; if we mark our presence in XYZ's party tonight; neither one of us will ever become suspects"; he doesn't stop but Will does. He turns around asks; "What about me?" I ignore him.

"Orleans that's the only way out, otherwise you know it's all over the school as well as social media that you and I are dating and that's a good enough evidence for police to connect my father's murder and my mother's skull injury to probably a blackmailed me and my frustrated boyfriend"; I pause; "and also you cursed my father's soul with the eternal sleep of you as his husband – that's just EXTRA!" by the time I come to my last word I know Orleans has stopped walking.
He takes his moment as his shoulders go high up and then down. He turns around, looks at me; he shakes his head and utter;
"First of all he deserves that and second fucking wash your hands and all the places where they've been to."

Vixxi- 20

We all know for a fact, that there is magic in names. Delicate, romantic and insatiable magic.

Best example: Highschool crushes; crushes built on bare moments, remembered by names. Like when the President of the school looks at you and nods in your direction acknowledging your presence. Like when the bad boy finds you sobbing and shows you his soft spot. Like when the homecoming queen out of the blue asks you to dance with her. Like when you suddenly have this urge to fix the slipping glasses of that geek girl who once tutored you maths. Like when you wanna put away that lock behind your first girlfriend's ears. Like when you want to wildly kiss your first boyfriend under a starry sky for several hours straight.

We all have been there, where we have snuck pictures of our crushes inside our pillow covers or made ship names or written letters or even worse, made portraits of them. And still today when there are no hidden pictures in our pillows, no remembrance of those love poems dedicated to them, nothing at all; we gush at their memories just by the call of their names.

When we adult, these names feel like an era in our lives. One name reminds you of spring, the other winter, one name reminds you of rain, the other thunder. Names carry that power. They carry memories; these memories carry stories; these stories carry feelings; and these feelings carry a lost time – a time to which you can go back and yet never go back.

Episode 47: Salem

Everything is clean.

I am sitting on the side of my bed staring at the open door, reviewing what happened today.

"He is in there; wanna see him for the last time?" Orleans enter my room.

My eyelids look up, my lips side pout. I nod and take a deep breath in.

"Where did you dig?" I took myself away when Orleans announced that it is the soil where my father will sleep. So I took off, I can't do all that digging in dirt – it's just not – clean?!!!

"Nobody will ever know where Mr. Enoch is buried – deep – deep down in the front lawn"; Orleans informs me as I stand and step to my bedside desk to take out my earphones.

I chuckle; "You gotta be kiddin' me – just because I don't have a backyard doesn't mean you will spoil my front yard"; I give him a side eye.

"What are you doing?" He asks looking at my fingers as I connect my earphones to my phone.

"I need music"; I roll my eyes; "Such a task!" I exhale. Orleans look at me with worry; "Ar – uh – Aren't we playing that *BGM maker* channel on the intercom already?" he does not understand me or my taste.

"Yea – but that was for cleaning stuff, now I want something so as to get my parent's signature on this little piece of paper which is the essential reason why all this fuck up started in the first place, right?" I press my lips into a plastic smile.

Orleans's forehead creases and his tilts his head gently in confusion; "Are we still getting those signed?" he asks.

"Yessss – we are still getting these signed. And now – I am definitely getting this signed. After these signatures; I will officially be the heir to everything that is under Enoch Enterprise – even your food cravings"; I grin side-ways as I speak those words.

Orleans's eyebrows rise in realisation.

I plug in my earphones; *Savage* by *Bahari* starts playing.

As I stand next to my death father's body all ready to be buried, I realise his death has still not hit me. For me all this is a music video and am just acting in it.

Savage still plays in the background; it is almost ending; I know the next song in my playlist. That song is my Love Anthem to my father.

Savage ends.

She wants me Dead by *Cazette* begins.

I bend down and get signature from a dead man's hand.

Episode 48: Orleans

"I can't. I can't. This – uh – What have I done?... What have I done? No no no no no – this wasn't how this was supposed to end... no no no..."; my lips keep mumbling, my legs wobble as I slide down the wall and crouch. My heart feels like it has a million knives digging into it. It can literally feel the cold edge of the knife pierce deep and deeper into it. My heart! My poor heart!

"Are you done?" Salem asks with the most frosty temperament. I look at her in bewilderment. How can someone be at such calm and cool. I just killed her father. How can she be forgiving and not try to kill me? I thought I knew Salem! To me I was sure that under all that calm and coolness lies her mechanic brain plotting ways to kill me inside the washroom.
I look directly into her eyes; she's still looking at me. When I lay my eyes directly into hers, I thought she would look away. But she did not, in fact her eyes are challenging me to look into her thoughts.
'Can you stop crying? It really isn't helping me at all'; and there I make contact. I drop my idea to talk to her and look away.
"No"; she speaks out loud. My head jerks back up at her; "What?" I ask in confusion.
"No"; she repeats her words.
"Talk to me"; she continues. I cover my face with my palms; "I am"; I feel exhausted, like I've been to war and back.
"No – not with sounds; talk to me as I am"; Salem begs. I slowly look in her direction, am astounded. Did she just say '*talk to me as I am*'? 'Cause that shit is some deep dramatic longing to be heard.
"What do you mean?" I ask her again to do away with my confusion. Salem can't be sentimental. She's a psychopath for all I know. (That or maybe she's just an angry kid)
"You can talk to me with words"; I do not like the idea of entering into her brain.
"Please. Just do it. I can't speak. It makes me – makes me –"; she gulps as she struggles to finish her sentence.
"Makes you feel vulnerable?" I help her out.

"Guilt? Weak? Human?" I help her some more. She gulps again, her eyes suddenly softens, water glistens and layers her lenses. Her pupils dilate, I can sense a sudden rush of anxiety increase in her body. She's a broken piece of biology begging to be fixed.
If she can't say her thoughts, fine I'll try listening to them.

Episode 49: Orleans

We are singularly the most helpless species. Ever.
'I'd do it all again. I'd kill him all again. I'd tape her too. She gave me what I don't deserve. So, I'd had to become stronger. And stronger and stronger. Strong until I was coarse as itching sand. I'm broken Orleans, do you think that I don't know that? Do you think I like killing my father. NO. I DON'T.
I have stopped having feelings. But you will kiss me. I think I love you. And the irony is that you can't even love me. It's alright – it's alright – it's alright. You see, karma is a bitch. I am torn Orleans. Please kill me. Please stab in my fucking stupid heart. I like being invisible, it is more invincible. When I am visible am more at fault. When am with you, I see how horrible I am. Yesterday – yesterday I didn't even care if I kill myself. Yesterday – I didn't even care if I need anything else. But today. Today I HAVE YOU. TODAY I HAVE A MIRROR. AND I HATE MYSELF. I hate it, Orleans. Please save me. Please kiss me. Please hug me. PLEASE. PLEASE PLEASE. FIGHT WITH ME. PLEASE CALL ME A BITCH. CALL ME A MURDERER. HUG ME ORLEANS!

Hug me like my mother never did. Hug me and remind me how my mother wasn't entirely at fault. Hug me and make me see good in my father. For once just kiss me and shake me and tell me – tell me that my father can still see me. Hug me Orleans! I need you. Don't leave me. I have never cried. And I am not crying. Right now am begging. Not a single tear have I shed. Not a single tear. But I can feel a lump in my throat, and I can feel a darkness cloud over my chest. I can feel a thunder rumble. Please, Orleans, please. I have no one. Why did you come? Had you not come to me. I'd be fine. I'd felt nothing. I've had no mirror to reflect from. Now I have you. My faults, my insanity all clear in your crystals. This is killing me. My mother did not train me for this. My father did not train me for this. Hell! Please kill me. I can't. No more. No more. This is how I feel. And I hate feelings. I am shaking. But I can't let you see. Can you read me? Please read me. I cannot confront my words. Oh yes, yes am afraid of my words. Here in this washroom. I have asked you to look at me and remain silent. I've asked you just stop and stare. Keep replying to my stare until I back away. I can't afford tears. I can't afford a single thing. But if you can read everything and all. Read this. Read this before I crumble and crush on listening my own words. I love you. And this isn't supposed to be me. But I love you. And I can't help loving you. This is the reason why I trust you. So please, yes please well your eyes and cry for me. Cry for those heard words that I've yet unsaid. Cry for those impossible words. Cry for me. Shed a tear for me. Please kiss me again Orleans. I am cursed cursed cursed and cursed, and the irony is that I am not even cursed. You are. Oh, Orleans how I wish, I wish to 'come straight. How I wish to express whatever I feel through you. How I wish to be you. To be like you. But I know I am doomed. I had been doomed ages ago. I am dead for my mother and my father just died. I let him be killed – it felt as if I killed him by my own hands. You saw that. Please, now kill me. Kill me Orleans! And be my saviour. Stop this misery. Please love me like no lover had. Send me to the stars.'

My tears have flooded my face. The salty water is dripping down my lips. She is stiff like a stick. Her mind stopped talking to me. There is a party outside but here, in this washroom, there is a funeral.

Not once did her eye blink. Not once did she cry out loud. On her face, not a single word is expressed. But here on mine, I am crying a river.

She exhales, rolls her eyes.

"Whoa! That was enough I guess"; she dare speak so casually! "Now get your ass up and help me cover our track. And also Yong's wish"; all her words come out of her mouth as if we just came out of a movie hall.

"What wish?"I ask her. I have no idea what she is talking of.

"She wants us to officially state that we are in a relationship"; she shrugs her shoulders.

"What? No." The very thought makes me vomit.

"Shut up and kiss me alright? We don't have any other choice. This is the only way we can guarantee witnesses to confirm our presence during father's murder"; it doesn't seem like she's feeling any kind of loss or remorse at all.

"I am NOT – absolutely NOT kissing you"; I get up to my feet and reinstate the negative possibility of me kissing her.

"Will you stop being such a drama bitch!" she pushes the door open and murmurs with a stifling smile; "You are such a cry baby. Anyone can make you cry anywhere. ANYTIME! Just drink some of that love potion. I bet it will take away all that pain of yours. Here take my hair strand, with that you just might fall in love with me" she scoffs and leaves me standing still in the middle of the bathroom.

"What the actual fuck!" this woman is crazy and she will – definitely WILL – make me crazy too, if I stay any longer with her.

I take out the love potion. The one which makes you fall in love with someone whom you cannot consciously. All you have to do is drink the potion and make your first contact with that person.

The little shiny bottle looks awfully happy and blue. This little dose – oh well! This dose has a whole story of its own. Interesting, right? Such an inanimate object has a story of its own. A single drop of it has changed hundreds of life. Most of them ended as tragedy, the others something better. If I use it, I might regret it. But even otherwise my options aren't any better.

All these years, the oppression, anger, filth, misery that I've ever felt under my skin for being whoever I am; today I felt it on my skin. On its very surface, in those seconds, my skin repelled my soul, it literally rejected it. In those seconds I felt those moments come alive when I wished to be normal, when I wished to have in my hand the power of a commoner.

Mr. Enoch's hate is not unknown, his was belt in the strike of a belt while others is felt in the burn of their stares. I am familiar with this feeling. Mentally I have fought it in and out.

But I had come to accept it. But today, today there was something in the physical abuse. They say if you are strong mentally, you can survive even the doomsday. But today, today felt so different.

Today I felt as if the whip of Mr. Enoch's belt will break my soul. I felt so weak, so weak – so so so so so so weak that I can't imagine sustaining another blow such as that.

Does this mean I am giving up? Does this mean that I quit? Have I already accepted my tragic destiny?

I close my eyes, another tear rolls down my face; "Why is life so fucked up?" I open them again and without thinking I open the small blue bottle take a drop of it on my tongue.

I guess I've chosen tragedy after all.

 I push the washroom door open and quickly tuck my hand in my pockets to avoid their contact with anyone else.

I look out for Salem.

A bunch of people stand in the room, all gathered in groups, chitchatting, happy and out of trouble. I notice Salem.

"SALEM!" I shout, my shout turning heads as my voice travels across the room.

"SALE –"; I am left midway from calling out her again as someone gives me a push from behind. I turn around and find Qnyev stumbling; "Am so sorry"; and apologising. He is trying to get to the bathroom door which I have blocked.

"I just have to enter the washroom. Am in a hurry!" he is begging me. Those eyes. OH! SUCH BEAUTIFUL! BEAUTIFUL EYES!

Huh? Wait. What?

"Can I enter with you?" my words come out before I realise.

Qnyev's eyes widen; "ummm – I gotta pee dude!" I can see his awkwardness surface.

He pushes his hips behind the doors and tries to shut the door.

"NO"; I yell.

"Dude! Seriously"; he gives me the weird eye.

I still have my hold on the door. For some apparent reason, I do not wish to leave the door and have him away from me.

"I need to talk to you about something. It's very, very important"; I have no idea what I have to talk to him that is so important that I cannot leave the door and let the poor guy pee in peace.

"Oh – ohkay!" he is scared. Definitely scared.

"How about we talk on this after I pee"; he presses his lips together and tries harder to let me leave the edge of the door.

 "Why were you calling me?" I hear Salem's voice behind me. I, very carefully – very, very, very carefully turn my head around without letting go off the door.

"What are you doing?" I can see her eyebrows wiggle in confusion.

"I – do-n't – exactly – know!" my eyes narrow as I realise that I am certainly clueless.

"I really need to pee Orleans!" Qnyev tries to pull the door close. "Let him pee you melodramatic piece of shit!" Salem stomps on my feet. My fingers leave the door. The door immediately closes while my fingers go to my feet in reflex.

"Why would you do that?" I cry out loud in pain.

"It was necessary"; she force smiles, turn around and starts to walk away.

As she walks away, I am suddenly reminded of my mission in mind. I stop my crying, follow her to the middle of the room.

"Salem!" I call her out loud, my voice resonating around the room once again. She stops. Turns around. I pace quickly toward her, inhale deeply, my eyes take a good look at her. I have to do this. I must.

"Help me!" I look directly into her eyes, trying to block her thoughts but am unable to.

'Do it. Kiss me now. Dumbo. Do it right now. We can sell this. Make it viral Orleans or be ready for a cold blooded death...'; she keeps on ranting, forcing me to kiss her. I take a huge gulp and close the space between us.

Yong cries out a loud gasp in the background as my lips touch Salem's; "I told you! I told you he wasn't gay. For gawd's sake he had Salem's red lip colour on his lips when they came out of the washroom. They were definetly making out in there!"

And we kissed.

And boy did I sell it! Oh yes I did!

The shouts in the background, the screams, the photo clicking, the snapchatting, I can sense it all. I can even sense Will photobombing as much as possible.

We break apart. Salem's eyes shone with excitement. My heart didn't even lose a single beat. I didn't feel a single rush of adrenaline – excitement – or whatever shit that makes our heart run a marathon. Am so gay. I swear.

Even after the love potion, I can't straight up myself. This is like next level tragedy.

No – not even a tragedy.

It's fucking asshole reality sticking to me like a curse.

Creak!

Somewhere in the background a door opened. Bathroom door. My head jerks around. It feels like a scene from a movie. Everything else blurs in the background. My senses heighten to capture just the creaking of the door. My feet leave for the sound, my heart start racing and finally the DJ played my love anthem.

All Too Well (Acapella version)

I suddenly feel such rush of emotions and I knew – and I knew in that moment, only he could hurt me so much so to become my first love. And I felt being hurt, hurt of too much love, hurt of an impending betrayal by love, hurt to realise that I am standing – right now, right here – on the bridge where two ends meet and I sing to myself:

A Blackhole is here;

A Universe is about.

Epilogue

"Is this the house you are talking about?"
"Umm – well it says so on my map Red"; Minnie looks at the map to double-check teh location, she doesn't want to make a mistake – AGAIN!
"Oh dear Satan! You are trembling like a poor cat on water"; Xanxia rolls her eyes as she breathes in her pipe and takes the map away from Minnie.
The red dot on the map stains this exact house.
Xanxia takes a clear look at it for a minute, something odd looms around the dot.
"Aah!" Xanxia sharply exhales at the realisation.
The red dot starts spreading on the yellow parchment paper.
"What is it Xanxia?" asks Red.
"Yes, yes what is it?" Minnie steps behind Xanxia's shoulder trying to take a look at the map. "Yikes!" a high-pitch yelp escapes Minnie's mouth. Xanxia turns around and gives Minnie a dead-pan look; Minnie has her hands over her mouth; "Why? – Why do you have to make things look far more dramatic than they are?" Xanxia sighs.
"If you care to share; I'd be delighted"; Red smiles sarcastically.
"It's the red dot. It's spreading. But the good news is the house is correct"; she looks at Minnie and smiles to one side; "Well done at last"; she tauntingly appreciates Minnie, who narrows her eyes and smiles in disgust.
"What does that mean? Do we know the location of the love potions or not?"

"Yes"; Minnie replies as she moves forward, her face looking at the Enoch mansion; "Yes we do have the location of the dead body but – "; her head drops down and she turns around. She looks at Red; it hasn't been much time since Red joined the committee. She still is unknown to what had happened to the previous person who was in her place. *Nwanvu.* She had to die to make a place for Red. It was important. *It had a purpose;* Minnie says to herself as she looks at Red.

"But what?' Red asks impatiently.

"But the man is no longer carrying the love of the love potion"; Minnie speaks looking into Red's perplexed eyes. "Something must have triggered the man's emotions; instead of embracing the love he must have felt disgust and that converted the love into hate"; Minnie completes.

"So does that mean they will remain forever in debt to us?" Red asks.

"No darling"; Xanxia intervenes as she makes a puff in her pipe; "It simply means the boy child we came here for will be out of immense tragedy"; she smiles. Red does not seem to be able to buy the tale her sisters spoke of.

"You'll understand"; Minnie sighs; "Let's get to work"; she snaps her finger and they vanish.

Down in the dungeons there is complete silence.

A flash of lightening! Poof! The three women appear in a blink as if they were always there.

"Xanxia – at it!" Minnie says as she holds up the map.

The house rumbles and there comes a crack in the floor. The stone comes out from the floor, along with a huge amount of soil. A whole mound of fresh soil and broken stone is made beside the spot where Xanxia magically dug.
Red looks inside the hole.
"How will we take his – his good stuff out?" Red gives them a weird look. She was still new to all this.
"You are so disgusted"; Minnie snickers as she checks out Red's bottled up tomato face.
Xanxia makes another puff as she gives Red a side-glance; "Believe me, we've done worse with people. And believe me gear yourself up for this job"; with that Xanxia steps back and finds a nice spot against the wall to lean on.
Minnie extracts an empty glass capsule and proffers it to Red.
Red looks at the capsule and her eyes widen.
"Go on"; Xanxia says from the shadow, clearly enjoying Red's scared and embarrassed face.
"What if I won't be able to do it?" Red gulps as she looks at Minnie.
Minnie presses her lips tight and gives Red a pitiful look; "Well – you'd have to one day, so better do it today than wait"; Minnie shrugs.
Red takes a long breath and pierces her lips; she slowly takes the bottle and leans inside the dug hole. Mr. Enoch lies freshly dead and covered with soil.
"He's still fresh, his goodies haven't all gone bad. Extract them quickly"; Minnie verbally asks to impede Red. She didn't like the amount of time she was taking and thinking on to complete the task. After all, Minnie wanted to attend the Moon gala tonight.

"Yes yes. On it"; Red murmurs as she hears Xanxia chuckle in the background. *Come on Ri, I know you can do this;* she says to herself. Red takes her gloves off; opens the empty capsule and starts using the extraction spell.

With her magic she unzips Mr. Enoch special goods and lay them bare in front of the company.

"That is some interesting stuff"; Xanxia takes a quick peep before she goes back to her standing position. Minnie giggles; "Oh please! that is disgustingly dead"; Red looks at the two women analysing the dead man's privates. "How is this even legal?" Red murmurs as she examines Mr. Enoch's privates.

"Umm – what do they say?" Minnie's eyebrows stitch as she's searching for some words in her brain; "yeah – they say a witch always has her promise"; she smiles in some sense of victory.

Red exhales, she has always known that she isn't strong enough for being a witch. This was the only reason why she wanted to become the part of Witch's Incomplete/Complete Debt Records Committee; to overcome her fear and show her parents and relatives that she was much more than a kind heart. She looks at the dead body and his dead private parts. The man's face is pathetically mushed, almost decapitated; he was without a doubt murdered and that too by some witch or wizard. *Definietly something with magic has killed* him; Red thinks to herself. No human would be able to bury something so nasty under the stones of these dungeons and not leave a clue of any breakage or blood of sorts.

"Could you please hurry up Red"; Minnie was becoming impatient.

"What do you think happened to him?" Red asks out of curiosity.

"Death and a very nasty crush injury"; Xanxia speaks from the shadow.

"Red, it's insignificant and unnecessary for us to know why a human must have taken the help of magic to kill this man and bury him without a clue in sight. We aren't here to give him justice or solve a mystery of any kind. We are here to just complete this family's debt and we should better be over with it"; Minnie tries to sound not rude but such actions can't disengage the cruel reality of the work.

"But what if it's not a human who took help of magic? What if it is some magical person himself?" Red asks in defiance.

"What nonsense?" Xanxia comments. Minnie raises her eyebrow. She takes a moment to not give a belittling reply.

"Red, that is impossible. No magical person has ever been able to cross Mahehean Wall after its inception. And all those were left beyond the Mahehean Wall were either deported back or killed. Don't you know that already?" Minnie were having her doubts with this one. Why had the committe chosen her after all? What was in Red that even she couldn't figure out? Why was she given one of the most important reputed positions of the magical community?

"Oh I know that. That's not what am saying I meant – "; she says but Xanxia interrupts Red as she emerges from the shadows; "Dear dead people you talk a lot"; Xanxia widens her eyes and there is a frown making it obvious how much bored she had become from Red's conversation. Xanxia snaps her fingers and Mr. Enoch's freshly dead corpse levitates. Xanxia snaps again and a white fluid leaves his privates and floats in the air directing itself inside the capsule. Once the capsule is filled Xanxia drops her hand and the body falls freely down with a thud.

"Next time if you decide to have a full fledged discussion on solving the mystery behind all the incomplete debts please inform me in prior, I'd better get more stash for my pipe"; she gives Red an irritated smile.

Minnie internally thanks Xanxia for getting the work complete. Red was becoming a pain in the ass. Red chews the inside of her cheeks as she again feels intimidated by Xanxia and embarrassed of her questions. "I'm sorry I didn't mean"; she apologises.

"Whatever"; Minnie snaps her fingers and suddenly the mound of soil starts floating and magically directs itself back into the pit. In no time, the dug up hole is filled and Mr. Enoch is once again buried under the cover of fresh earthly soil and dungeon stones.

"Now we gotta get these babies into mumma oven, and this time Red, you better prove yourself worthy of the position you are designated"; Minnie snaps again her finger and vanishes in no time. Xanxia follows her. Red sighs in shame and sadness, she looks at the sperm bottle. "I hate this feeling"; she growls under her breath before she teleports herself to the master bedroom of the house. Mrs. Enoch is in her bed, deep asleep but the blankets have been pulled off from her. "This is so illegal"; Red says under her breath.
"Come on – get it done with"; Minnie impatiently says. Red takes a moment again; all this is just so ethically unsound, but she has to do this. She hesitantly moves forward; takes Mrs. Enoch's thighs apart, pulls off her panties and very unwillingly and hesitantly inserts the capsule inside her. Why – why does her job requirement states *completion of debt at all costs* – why??? Why can't there be incomplete debts? Why was this necessary? These questions flooded her mind as she completes the job. The moment the capsule is fully inserted in Mrs. Enoch; Red exhales. Thank the Magic that it exits otherwise if she were to commit this with her bare hands, she'd had died.
"Very well"; Minnie comes forward and waves her fingers. Mrs. Enoch is back as she were supposed to be in her bed lying deep asleep like doll. She'd been tortured, almost killed, widowed, had her memories erased and magically-mechanically raped all in one day and ironically she was still to be blamed for all the bad things that were to come at her.

None of the three witches in the room knew of anything that had happened in the house. All they cared about was the fulfilment of the debt that is recorded in the accounts of the witch embassy. Their task is done here.
Red sighs and Xanxia smirks; "Now all we wait is for nine months and the boy baby will be ours"
"How are you so sure it will be a boy?" Red's brow curves in confusion.
"Because I artificially separated the Y-chromosome carrying sperms"; she shrugs as breathes in her pipe.
"How will we know that she has conceived?" Red asks another question.
"Oh, that's the capsules job"; Minnie puts her hand over Red's shoulder; she squeezes very gently to reassure her. Red smiles and nods.
"Now let's go ladies"; Minnie looks at the map for another red dot and *snap!*
They vanish into thin air.

Fin.

www.ingramcontent.com/pod-product-compliance
Lightning Source LLC
Chambersburg PA
CBHW030917060726
47591CB00005B/1576